Jacob

Joe Baldwin

Copyright © 2020 Joe Baldwin

All rights reserved.

This is a work of fiction. Names, characters, places, and incidents either are the product of the author's imagination or are used fictitiously. Any resemblance to actual persons, living or dead, events, or locales is entirely coincidental

For those who have dealt with bullying.

You are the strong one.

Part I

Chapter 1

2019

Jacob Simeon entered his home and slowly closed the front door by pulling the handle down and placing the door in its frame. He released the handle, making minimal noise. His book bag was heavy on his shoulders. His remaining books were wrapped in his arms holding them to his small chest. His day at school, like every other day, was filled with studying and bullying. He was happy to be home where he could escape into his homework, unless his father was having a bad day.

Bernie Simeon was snoring away on the red recliner, which was ripped on the sides, the flaps hanging down like a shocked face. Jacob kept his blue book bag, with Captain America's shield sewn to the front, hanging on his back. He pulled the remaining books in his arms closer to his chest. He slid his dirty, broken white sneakers off and softly slid across the wood floor.

This was a game Jacob played every day. It was the try-not-to-wake-your-father game. Jacob's breathing evened out when he reached his bedroom door. But the stack of books was too much for him. The top textbook slid off and hit the floor. His father sounded like he was awakening from an exorcism. Coughing and wheezing breaths emitted from his throat.

"What's the matter with you!" his father screamed, catching his breath.

"I'm…I'm sorry, Dad," Jacob said, leaning down to retrieve his book. "It was an accident."

"It's fine, son. Come on. Come over here and sit down."

Jacob reluctantly wandered over but didn't sit. He stood at the side of the chair where his dad was attempting to recover his breathing.

"You just know your pops has got a weak heart, so you can't be doin' stuff like that."

Jacob frowned and stood and stared at the ground. Jacob could hear his father's breathing squealing from his nose as the man spoke.

"How was school today?"

Jacob shrugged his shoulders and tilted his head to the right.

"That's the answer I get every damn day from you," Bernie said.

"That's how my days go," Jacob responded.

"Is something going on at school? Any kids picking on you?"

He asked this same question every time Jacob lost the don't-wake-your-father game. It was like the consolation prize. Of course, he was being picked on constantly. He'd gotten shoved into lockers. He'd gotten crumpled papers thrown at the back of his head in the middle of class, and when he unraveled them, they read, "Nerd," with a drawing of a dick underneath. He had even gotten his head dunked into a toilet full of shit.

If he told his father this, he couldn't—wouldn't—do anything about it, and if he did do something about it, it would only look like his daddy coming to the rescue.

"Nah, just school stuff," Jacob said finally.

Bernie gave him a look like he didn't believe him, and said, "All right, but you know what to do if someone hits you or pushes you around, right?" Bernie had been teaching him boxing when he came home with a purple marking around his eye that looked like a purple pond around the island of eyeball. Jacob was always good about hiding his markings from his father. He had said he was late for class and as he was running down the stairs he tripped on his untied shoelace and hit his face on the railing. But Bernie didn't buy that story and was excited to teach his son self-defense.

The real reason for the bruise around the eye was Robbie Stan. Robbie had been messing with Jacob ever since Robbie first saw him. They passed in the hall on the first day of school, and Robbie tripped him, forcing his book bag to flip over his head and smacking his face on the green, linoleum floor. Luckily, there was no visible damage that time—only a bloody nose that had stopped before he got home—so he didn't need to explain anything to his father. But Jacob wasn't lying about the marking on around his eye. He did hit a railing face first. It just wasn't at school, and he was pushed.

"Stand up," Bernie said.

Bernie stood and so did Jacob.

"Now place your hands in fists in front of you."

Jacob made two fists and was standing with his feet close together.

"First of all, spread your feet," Bernie said and kicked Jacob in both shins. "Secondly, place your thumbs on the outside of your other fingers."

Jacob did so.

"Okay, now hit me," Bernie said.

Jacob threw a punch into his father's gut. Jacob's hands were shaking.

"That's all you got? Why do you hit like a girl? Let me show you." Bernie got onto his knees and shot a jab into Jacob's stomach. Jacob held his midsection and sat on the couch fighting back the tears. "That didn't hurt. Stop being a crybaby. Get up and—"

Luckily, there was a soft rapping on the front door. Bernie walked over and answered it.

"Carrie, what are you doing here?" Bernie exclaimed, surprised to see her.

Carrie had cornrows on the right side of her head, and the left side was straight dark hair that flowed down past her shoulders. She had a blue blouse that tied in bow at the front with a white floral pattern. She had jean shorts even though it was the end of September.

"I was in the neighborhood and wanted to check in on my favorite nephew," she said, walking over to him with her lips pursed. But Bernie held his large arm out like a barrier.

"Well, he doesn't wanna see you."

Carrie shoved his arm out of the way, ignoring him. She lifted Jacob up and planted a kiss on his forehead. It left a red mark. Jacob always hated lipstick marks but loved kisses and hugs. Especially since his mother had left. As she lifted him, he winced.

"What's wrong, sweetheart?" she asked him. Jacob only sat back on the couch, staring at the ground.

"All right, you saw him. Now you can go." Bernie's booming voice came from behind her.

"Jacob, honey, head up to your room. I need to speak with your father in private," Aunt Carrie said.

Jacob ran up the stairs but remained peeking through the balustrades at the top landing.

"Are you beating up your son?" Carrie said in a low voice.

"That's ridiculous," Bernie said.

"Well, my sister, *your* wife, has been missing for a year today," Carrie said

"Okay, and what's your point?"

"My point is what did you do to her? Because if you have no problem beating on a little kid, you certainly wouldn't mind doing it to a grown woman," Carrie said emphatically.

Bernie rolled his eyes and sat on the couch, cracking open a beer.

"What happened to you? You loved her. What happened?" Bernie only sat on the worn couch and shrugged his shoulders.

Carrie moved her head slowly from left to right. "You're unbelievable." She continued. "I mean, beer cans everywhere, clothes covering the floor." She walked around the home. "Brenda would have never let you keep it like this, and she wouldn't want her son living that way either."

That triggered something in Bernie. He shot up from the couch and went to place his hand around the neck of Carrie. Jacob gasped, and it echoed down. They both simultaneously looked up at him. Then Carrie stared into Bernie's eyes. "I wish you would," she said with contempt.

Carrie turned from him and walked upstairs to where Jacob was sitting on the landing. "If you ever get too scared or unhealthy, just call me and you can live with me, okay?" she said, sitting at Jacob's level.

Jacob only sat there, shaking like he was cold, but he was scared. He had seen his father be mean before, but it still made him nervous.

"Okay. Promise me," she said again.

"I promise," he said in a choked voice.

She planted another kiss on his forehead, leaving another mark. Jacob watched her walk down the stairs and out the door but giving Bernie a dirty look prior to leaving.

"Crazy fucking woman," Bernie muttered to himself. "Jacob, get down here!"

Jacob ran into his room and slammed the door. He wished there was a lock on his door. Instead, he scraped his dresser across the floor, placing it in front. But it didn't matter because his father stayed downstairs for the rest of the night. Jacob finished his homework and colored the comic book he'd created.

Chapter 2

2008

"Push, Misus Williams, push!" the doctor willed her. He stood on her right side in a stainless white lab coat, a comforting hand on her shoulder. But Brenda Williams didn't find it comforting at all. Her head and upper back were lifted off the bed, and she was using every ounce of energy she had left to push this big baby's head out of her finally. They had been at this for nearly an hour now.

"You're doin' great, honey." Her boyfriend Bernie Simeon, who had stayed by her side through the whole pregnancy, was there with a blue hair cap. A blue surgeon mask looped in his ears, covering his mouth and nose, and a white gown draped over him, tied at the back. He was keeping her awake and cheering her on.

The baby had wanted to come into the world quickly—one month before the due date—but now it was being stubborn. Brenda had woken in the middle of the night, slapping Bernie to wake him screaming about frequent contractions.

"They're only a few minutes apart," she had said.

Bernie, with his eyes barely opened, was standing before he even recognized he was standing, and grabbed the baby carrier they had kept in their bedroom.

He walked down the stairs and entered his Dodge Ram, threw the carrier in the rear cab, and started the engine. It roared to life, and he reversed out of the driveway, only to fully wake up and notice his wife not in the passenger seat.

He gently walked her down the stairs and to his truck, and he went fifty-five in a twenty-five-mile-per-hour zone, blowing through red lights, getting to the nearby hospital in two minutes on a normal ten-minute drive in the early morning hours. The baby was coming so quickly they had no time to prepare for a cesarean delivery. They wheeled her to the delivery room and pumped pain drugs into her blood intravenously, telling her to push.

The doctor playing catch at the exit point seemed to be a mile away to Brenda and kept moving further away. She wasn't sure if it was the drugs or the loss of oxygen, but the doctor drifted to the other side of the room, with his voice saying, "You are doing awesome, just a bit more." He sounded more like he was at the end of a tunnel, and it echoed to her ears. She could feel the beads of sweat flowing down her nose and cheeks dripping onto her cleavage. She was extremely light-headed and informed the doctor she was going to pass out. The doctor only told her again how great she was doing. She was so tired of hearing that phrase.

"You won't pass out, my dear. I'll make sure of it." The doctor to her right assured her. He seemed to be in charge, as he was instructing the nurses and doctors in the room on what to do.

"Here it comes," the doctor playing catch said. He froze for a moment and gave a worried look to the head doctor. The black man in the white coat whipped to the exit point, sat in a chair on wheels with no back.

"Dr. Jones, clear the room and call a pediatric code blue."

"Is something wrong?" Brenda asked in a panting breath.

"No, of course not," he said as an announcement blared over the PA system: "All available nurses report to Room forty-five." He slowly reached a hand into the vagina and slowly pulled the baby's feet, which were coming out first.

Brenda screamed in pain. "What the fuck is happening?" she wailed.

"Get everyone out of here who doesn't need to be here. Now." The doctor was now yelling at his colleague.

"Okay, everyone, let's give her some room and take a breather outside," he said in a shaky, hushed voice. Bernie ignored the nervous doctor's orders and pushed toward Brenda. The doctor laid a hand on his shoulder to gently lead him the opposite way.

Bernie knocked his hand off his shoulder. "I'm not goin' anywhere until you tell me what's wrong with my girl and my baby."

"Everything's fine. Now if you could just—" The doctor, who looked to be a resident, attempted again to lead him away from her.

"Stop fucking touching me, and clearly everything is not okay. I'm not stupid. Now tell me what the fuck has happened. This is my kid you're driving me away from." They had a stare down for a few seconds. Then the doctor sighed, and just as he opened his mouth to speak, a team of four nurses rushed into the room and surrounded his wife.

Brenda's screams had stopped, and she looked to be unconscious but still breathing. The head doctor informed the team, "The feet are coming out first, and it appears we have a nuchal cord; I'm going to slide the infant out slowly and slide two fingers between the cord and the baby's throat."

Bernie stood in shocked silence. He was frozen, tears falling down his cheeks.

"We should go. Let them do their job," the doctor said, this time keeping his hands to himself. One of the nurses pulled the white shower curtain closed, and Bernie slowly backed out of the room, not blinking once.

***

The doctor emerged from behind the large double bay doors. Bernie scrambled to his feet and rushed over to him. His white trench coat was now covered in red splatters.

"My baby…my Brenda. Wha-what happened?"

19

The doctor looked at him with a serious expression. "Why don't you take a seat, Mr. Simeon." The doctor motioned for the hard, blue waiting room seats.

"I've been sitting for the past three hours. Tell me if my family is okay," Bernie said, not noticing he was swaying a bit. The doctor placed his hands out in front of him.

"Your wife will be fine. But your son—"

"My son, I have a son. A boy, I can't believe it." Bernie and Brenda had wanted to be surprised by the gender.

"Yes, well, he's currently in the pediatric ICU. When he was in the womb, the umbilical cord had wrapped tightly around his windpipe. We estimate he hadn't been able to breathe for several minutes. My team members are currently performing every lifesaving measure possible."

Bernie noticed he was now swaying, and he attempted to keep his balance, but he fell backward into one of the hard, plastic waiting room chairs.

The doctor comforted him and said, "However, you are free to visit your girlfriend."

***

Bernie woke to a nurse gently rubbing his arm. His butt was hanging over the side of the small hospital bed, being the big spoon to Brenda, who was taking up most of it.

"Mr. Simeon, you can see your little boy now. I don't know if you want to wake your wife," the nurse whispered.

"She's not my wife, only my girlfriend." Bernie didn't know why that was pertinent information to give at this time, but that was what came out from his sleeping stupor.

The nurse nodded her head with a look of apology painted on her face.

Bernie slowly dropped off the bed to his feet and followed the nurse to the hallway. Bernie had so many thoughts running through his head. *Is my son alive? Can I hold him in my arms?* This was something he had been dreaming of doing for the past eight months.

He passed by rooms of sleeping women who had just been through birth or were waiting their turn. Bernie hoped nothing like what happened to him would happen to any of these families.

The nurse swiped her key card on a card scanner, opening large double doors to an area with windows on the left side. Behind the glass were cradles of infants lined in rows. She led him to the end of the hallway. Bernie was far behind looking at every baby hooked up to a machine to stay alive.

"The one all the way at the top," she said, placing her finger at the top of the window. Bernie saw his son's face for the first time, and he had noticed he had Brenda's eyes and his big head.

"Can I hold him?" he asked.

"Unfortunately, he needs to remain on the breathing machine for now, but we expect him to recover just fine and breathe on his own and live a normal life." He was so small.

"Is he a normal size…and everything?" Bernie didn't understand much of what she was saying or anything medical for that matter.

"He was premature, so he'll be a bit lighter than normal, but just follow what the doctor says, and your boy will be just fine."

"Thank you," Bernie said and hugged her. She wasn't expecting it but embraced him anyway.

Chapter 3

2019

Jacob was woken from a desk nap by the thudding sound of a door and two different voices that floated into his room. The red digital numbers on the clock he kept on his bedside table read 2:34 a.m. Jacob peeled the paper that was stuck to the side of his face.

"Fuck," Jacob muttered to himself. The wet stain in the center of the comic strip Jacob was working on had soaked into the page. Jacob had always drooled when he slept. His mother had had to change his pillowcase daily because he'd found it uncomfortable to sleep in his own saliva.

The colored pencil that he was using to shade now looked as though he were working with watercolors. Luckily, he didn't stack the rest of his work underneath this one. Jacob reached into the top right drawer of his desk pulling a single sheet of paper from the drawer and began to draw the page over again. This was the final page of the comic he'd created, but he still had half of the fourteen pages to color in.

Jacob was so pleased with what he had accomplished that he read his unfinished work from the beginning. He had always doodled on the side of his notes during a boring class or when he couldn't get up from his bed on the weekends, but this was the first official comic he'd created. And moreover, he could win tickets to GreenCon, the comic convention that took place here in the city. But Jacob knew his father would never let him go due to his disdain for comics. He didn't much care, though. He more so wanted the part of the prize where they hung your work in the main hallway for the rest of the school year.

Being in awe of his work, he brought over the first thirteen pages he kept in his bedside drawer to hide from his dad. Bernie once found a comic book, and he treated it as if it were a porn magazine. He had said comic books were for gay little white boys and not a strong black man like he said Jacob was. After that, Jacob hid his small collection (mostly from his mother) inside a cardboard box underneath his bed. He knew his father wouldn't look there because he barely came into his room at all.

He sat at his desk, flipping the pages over, reading through them. The first seven pages were drawn and colored, and Jacob had a tear drop from his eye because of how happy he was the way it had come out. He loved the character he'd created—Captain Ember, the defender of earth's sun. He wore a spandex suit that was orange from the legs up to the chest which bled into a red flame. Jacob didn't want to draw an outline of a penis, so he decided there would be no genitalia.

His powers included throwing fire from his hands and mouth, the strength of a million men, and flying at hundreds of miles per hour. And most importantly, no cape.

Captain Ember's story began when he was a Captain Charles of the United States Army. He was sent by higher ranking officials on a top secret mission to take down an enemy. Local police in the area called him Ice Man. Ice Man was said to be robbing banks by using a freezing device to open safes; he'd stolen millions of dollars.

The Ice Man had now released a video talking about his biggest job yet—taking down the president of the United States. Captain Charles tracked his location down to a facility where they made hot wax.

He entered and instructed his team to spread out to locate the enemy. The team of eight men eventually ended up on the metal catwalk that overlooked the facility. Ice Man was found in a dark corner, and the captain approached him. Ice Man had a blanket draped over his shoulders and white steam floated from the pores of his skin. When the captain got close enough, he could see that he had a suit on. It looked to be more like a costume: a white bodysuit with thin blue lines like veins running through the entirety of it.

The blue streaks lit up, and Ice Man threw his arms in front of him. Three giant icicles flew at the captain. He dove out of the way, only to be hanging off the catwalk, dangling over one of the hot wax vats.

The captain now knew he was dealing with a supernatural being. His team approached each side of Ice Man with their guns drawn. He shot more icicles at the men, knocking the guns from their hands to the floor below. He stood over the captain, smiling. He placed his hands on the fingers holding the captain from falling. Ice

Man created ice around his hands and the metal bar. The ice was now holding him there.

One of the army men told him to freeze, and he only laughed. A large glacier that exceeded the width of the catwalk sailed toward the army personnel. Two of the men ducked, and one bailed over the side, falling to his death.

Ice Man said goodbye and jumped off the catwalk, creating a slide of ice as he did and exiting the factory. The captain began to feel drips of water on face from the melting ice. Then the ice cracked, sending him into the pool of hot wax. The two army men on the catwalk watched him fall after missing catching him.

The last frame was his hand sinking in. Weeks later, he shocked doctors by waking in the hospital with not a burn on him. He was sent home and soon found out he could shoot fire from his hands and mouth. He could even levitate with flames underneath him like a jet pack. His first order of business was to take down Ice Man.

Jacob had drawn out the words "Pick up the next issue of Captain Ember soon." As he had seen many other comic books do.

Jacob continued with the drawings of lines of lead across the page, sending out an audible scraping sound. He was doing this as discreetly as possible. The laughter coming from the living room was getting on his nerves, but if his father had caught him awake at this time, he would surely get a beating.

Jacob had never heard this woman's voice before. His father had been bringing different women home since his mother had left them.

Eventually, Jacob got curious and wanted to see what his next possible mother would look like. He shuffled across the floor in his socks, avoiding the parts of his hardwood floor that made a creaking noise. He softly got to his knees and peeked through the keyhole that looked out at the bottom of the couch. He could only see their legs dangling. He could hear what they were saying in muffled voices but didn't much care what they were talking about.

He saw his father in the only pair of dress pants he owned, a beige pair of khakis he wore during his own mother's funeral, but also wore to barbecues. The woman had a short dress on and shoes with a big heel, both hot pink in color.

The woman straddled his father's lap, and her dress slipped up on its own revealing two large dark humps and a hot pink fabric flossing her ass crack. The lip smacking and moaning was making Jacob nauseated, so he returned to his drawing.

When the door to the room next to his slammed shut and the thin walls made the noises more vocal, he went over to his bedside drawer and pulled out a pair of over-the-ear headphones. He plugged the other end into his iPod Touch he'd bought—along with the headphones—with the money he'd earned from helping Alex's parents with chores around their house. Jacob did chores at his father's home, but there was no way he was earning money from it.

He didn't have many songs downloaded, but he tapped on Tony Terry singing soulfully about being "With You." He learned this music from his mother, whom he wished he could be with right now.

Chapter 4

2009

Brenda and Bernie were having a hard time keeping a straight face every time they saw the waiter headed in their direction with the clear plastic pitcher of water. He was filling their glasses to the rim even after a small sip was missing. As the waiter whipped around the corner out of sight, they broke into a fit of laughter, and Bernie reached across the small table and grabbed her hands.

The Chinese decorations flooded the room with black symbols on red accordion decorations. The laughing calmed down, and Bernie was staring at her, not moving anything on his face, just staring.

"What?" she said shyly.

"You are so damn beautiful," he said as she hovered her hands over her eyes. He gently grabbed her wrists to pull them away.

"Hey, let me see that gorgeous face. I miss it," he said as tears formed in her eyes.

"Are you okay?" he asked in a hushed tone.

A new couple walked in the front door, and the host rushed them to the table behind Bernie.

"Yes, I've just never had someone be so kind to me before." She was fanning her face with her hands so as not to smudge her makeup she'd applied carefully for thirty minutes before heading out. Bernie had placed Jacob down for a nap and quietly suggested they go to dinner. It was something they hadn't done since the birth three months prior.

"Are you kidding me? I'll be right there." Brenda's sister Carrie had said before Brenda even had to ask. Luckily, she was only a five-minute drive away.

"Well, you are the most beautiful human being on this earth inside and out," Bernie said taking her hands again, but she pulled away to take a sip of water and wipe the tears that came again.

"I actually got you a little something." Bernie said as the waiter rushed over with the water pitcher to drop a dash of water into Brenda's cup.

"Aw, Bern, you don't need to get me any—" He placed his hand out, his palm facing her.

"I insist."

Bernie squeaked his chair backward and stood up.

"Where are you going?" Brenda asked horrified as her boyfriend climbed onto the seat of his chair and then onto the table, spreading his feet just inches away from their unfinished food.

"Oh my god, Bernie, get down," she said, embarrassed.

"May I have everyone's attention, please," he yelled across the small restaurant.

An elderly couple looked up from their soup with a tight-lipped disapproval. The young couple that had just walked in glanced up from their menus and then went back to searching for the food they want. The waiter with the glass pitcher rushed in, and a small grin creased his face.

"Oh my God, get down," she whispered, covering her face and tugging at the bottom of his pant leg. The table he was standing atop was not sturdy, and he needed to find the right balance, like a beginner trying to surf for the first time. Before he could find his balance, he tilted the table enough for their forks and knives to fall to the floor.

"This woman right here is my beautiful girlfriend, and we went on our first date one year ago today." Bernie's booming voice pulsated through the small restaurant.

A few of the patrons gave an unenthusiastic patter of applause.

"Thank you. And we just had a handsome baby boy three months ago."

The elderly couple glanced at each other with raised eyebrows.

"That's right, we got it on early," he said, moving his hips a bit, and the table moved again, but he found his balance. A few chuckles and nervous coughs could be heard from the customers.

Brenda stood tugging at his striped polo shirt and told him to get down now. But he ignored her and continued. She had never been so embarrassed in her entire life.

"I've only been with her for one year." Brenda covered both sides of her face and started walking to the exit. "But I already know I wanna spend the rest of my days with her."

She stopped and turned to see him hopping off the table and embracing her. He dropped to his right knee and removed a small box from his khaki pants pocket. He opened the box to reveal a princess cut silver diamond ring that glistened in the strong restaurant lighting.

Brenda gasped and cupped a hand over her mouth along with the old woman at the table to her right.

"Brenda Williams, will you marry—" He couldn't finish because her mouth was on his. They kissed passionately for a few seconds that ended with a loud smooching sound.

"I guess she said yes," he said as she pulled away.

The few customers roared with applause. He placed the ring on her shaking left ring finger and the fit was perfect, and so was she.

Chapter 5

2019

Jacob opened his eyes yet again, and a jazzy saxophone vibrated in his ear, almost euphorically. He noticed sunlight gleaming through the blinds sitting on his only window. He frantically scrambled when he glanced at his bedside clock and it read 10:00 a.m. School was almost halfway over. He peered down at his half-colored comic, and his body went cold, knowing the school contest was due in two hours. There was no way he would finish in time. He would need to sneak in some coloring during classes. And he didn't have a free period or a study hall on Fridays.

When he stared at himself in the bathroom mirror, he almost forgot he still had the marking by way of Robbie. It was fading a bit, but still prominent. He opened the mirror cabinet that sat adjacent to the sink. Hidden behind pill bottles and lotions was a small black bag with "Brenda" written in faded red lipstick. His mother had left this makeup bag when she'd run off a year ago without saying a word. Jacob unzipped the bag and removed the small bottle of concealer and spread it onto the area. He winced as he used his finger to blend the dark color to match his skin color. His mother and him had the same skin tone. Jacob smiled at that thought.

It looked good as new. He usually called it his *new* face. Luckily, he never had anyone accidentally bump his face revealing the bruises. But sleeping typically wiped it off when he moved on his pillow or slept on his arm at his desk, so he needed to reapply nearly every morning.

Jacob stared at his reflection for a few seconds. He wished he had a different face, one that wasn't ugly. He also wished he had a different body, one that wasn't so flabby. And maybe the kids wouldn't call him Jabba the Hutt. He didn't know who that was, but his mother had said it was from an old movie and not to worry about it. He mostly just wanted to stay in bed and lock the door for the rest of his life, that would make him the happiest. Jacob quickly slid his unfinished work into his Superman book bag. He threw his favorite shirt over his head. It showed the Batmobile with Joker on top, zooming down the streets of Gotham. He always remembered watching old episodes of *Batman: The Animated Series* with his mom. It was a show that was on in the '90's, but Jacob's mom had gotten it on DVD for him because she thought he may enjoy it. As always, Mom was right. She had always encouraged him to chase his dreams.

"If you wanna draw your little characters and if that's what you wanna do when you grow up, then you go for it, sweetie," she had said, rustling his hair.

Jacob tiptoed in his white sneakers—with the bottoms half falling off—into the living room. He wore his book bag slung over one shoulder. The door of his father's bedroom was shut all the way. It was like this every morning. He always sneaked by to catch the bus.

Unfortunately, today, the bus was long gone, and he needed to wake his father up to drive him to school. Jacob's shaking hand reached for the door handle and slowly turned it. The first view he had was two black balloons one on top of the other. He covered his eyes with his hands, peering through his fingers to see where he was going.

He walked around to the other side of the bed where his father was snoring, facing the wall away from his naked woman friend. Jacob tapped him on the forehead with one finger, but he just continued to enjoy dreamland. Jacob then did something his father said his brother and him did to each other when they were younger. Jacob squeezed his father's nostrils together. Bernie snorted and coughed; his eyes shot open. His eyes were bloodshot, and he continued to hack as he sat up.

"I need a ride to school, it starts in five minutes," Jacob said.

"Wh-what?" Bernie mumbled, still not fully awake.

"I missed the bus, and I'm late for school," Jacob pleaded with him.

"Just take the school bus, the yellow one." Bernie's mumbling was getting worse. Then his head fell back to the pillow.

Jacob stared at him, wondering if he should do the nostril trick again. Just as he went to turn away, his father's large hand shot out and wrapped around his throat. Jacob pounded his father's wrist and forearm. His book bag dropped to the ground, and he was slowly being lifted off the ground. Jacob was trying to scream. Maybe the woman in the bed would be able to hear him, but no noise came from him. Bernie's eyes were only slits and his face stoic.

"You leave again, Imma fuck your shit up." Bernie muttered as Jacob was losing air and life.

Jacob was feeling lightheaded and weak. He had no strength to fight back. Jacob closed his eyes to go to sleep and forget everything, just wait for the end, which comforted him. Blackness took over his brain. His father was shouting more obscenities but was only a fading sound in his mind.

Then a pain shot up his spine, and he could breathe again. He was on the bedroom's hardwood floor, lying on his side. Bernie's snores and the soft breathing of the woman became clear again. Jacob grabbed his book bag and ran out of the room, leaving the door open. He exited the front door, shutting it softly, and began his walk to school.

Chapter 6

2014

Brenda and her sister Carrie shared the same birthday, but they weren't twins. They were exactly one year apart. But that didn't stop them from telling everyone who asked that they are identical twins, which they looked and felt like. They felt they had the power of telepathy growing up. Sometimes they would be thinking the same thing at the same time and answering questions at the same time. It was their party trick.

"Where's the birthday boy? I haven't seen him since I got here," Carrie asked across the large wooden dining room table which had "Happy 6th Birthday" balloons floating smoothly in the gust of the overhead kitchen fans. A round cake sat uncut in the middle of the table.

"He won't leave his room. Bernie had to pick him up and physically place him in the car for school the other day. I don't know what's gotten into him lately," Brenda said, slicing a piece of cake. The knife slid through the round cake, cutting a triangular slice.

Carrie slapped her hand and Brenda snapped her hand to herself, scoffing at her sister. "We are waiting for Jacob. He gets the first slice." Carrie scowled in Brenda's direction. "Is everything okay at school? Is he bullied?" Carrie asked, going back to the original conversation.

Brenda shrugged her shoulders. "Not that I'm aware of, but a black child who loves superheroes and drawing is bound to be bullied at some point."

Carrie nodded her head in agreement.

"Prying information out of his safe of a mind is near impossible," Brenda continued, "but I hear he does have a friend named Alex."

"Well, that's good. One good friend equals a million bad ones if you ask me," Carrie said, taking a sip out of her glass of red wine.

"Even our punter is faster than your fa-fastest running back or receiver." The swoosh of the rear sliding door sounded before Bernie's booming voice entered the kitchen where Brenda and Carrie sat. He talked about football all the time with his drinking buddy, Jackson, especially in November.

"What are you even talking about?" Jackson said in return. They both held skinny beer bottles. Jackson was a professional body builder, and Brenda always found particularly attractive Jackson's shapely jaw and the arms stretching out the small shirts he wore. He was also kind and not an alcoholic. Bernie had large arms as well, but his beer belly gave away it was only fat.

"How many are you on, Bernie?" Brenda asked in a firm tone.

"This is my second one." This was always his answer, no matter if she saw him take three or more.

"Mm-hmm," she responded. The party was ending without a show of the birthday boy.

"He's stillnhisrm?" Bernie asked, slurring his last couple words.

Brenda and Carrie nodded at the same time.

"He won't come out." Carrie said.

Bernie marched to Jacob's room and pounded a fist into the wooden door.

"You get out here right now, boy. Your family came all this way to see you. And you're being really fucking rude!" Bernie yelled, banging the door continuously.

Brenda moved swiftly behind him and hugged him, wrapping her arms around his waist.

"Honey, it's his birthday. If he wants to stay in his room all day, then you should let him," she said softly into his ear.

"No, I refuse to have a disrespectful son." Bernie took a few steps back to the opposite wall. He pushed his leg up and forward, and the door let out a loud crack. The door was intact, but a sliver ran in a zigzag motion down the center like a line on a map that separated states.

Brenda grabbed his large arm and attempted with all her strength to pull him away. "Bernie, stop. Please stop."

But the size-thirteen boot went up again, and the door exploded in half. Jacob was on his bed cross-legged with a comic book open on his lap. He cowered into the corner of his bed and the wall. He was trapped, and the only protection was his arm he held out over his head. Bernie dropped the beer bottle, and it shattered. Dark liquid flowed in every direction between the broken glass.

Bernie reared his arm back, his hand balled into a fist. He brought it down upon Jacob.

Whack! Suddenly, Brenda's face appeared between the two and fell to the ground with a thud. Bernie immediately dropped to his knees in another thud. His mouth hung open, and he was visibly shaken.

"Brenda. Wake up, sweetheart," he said stroking her hair and gently caressing the purple bruise forming on her cheek. He looked over his shoulder at Jackson. "Get an ice pack from the freezer."

But Jackson had backed out of the room and fled from the home already. It was only Carrie standing inches behind him in the room now. Carrie pushed him, and he lost his balance, falling to the ground and staring at the ceiling. Carrie was now crying and comforting her sister in her arms.

"Let me help," Bernie said, climbing back to his knees.

"Get the fuck out." Carrie never had to raise her voice in her thirty-two years of life until now.

"Look, I just want—"

Carrie placed her palm at his face and he stopped. "I said, get the fuck outta here," she said, pointing to the exit.

"Kicked out of my own house," he muttered, exiting. The slam of the front door indicated he'd left. Carrie waved Jacob over, and he pulled himself up from being pressed as far against the wall he could.

"Are you all right, Jacob?"

Jacob softly nodded his crying face and felt comforted in his aunt's arms. All three of them embraced as Brenda came to.

Chapter 7

2019

The neighborhood Jacob and his father lived was the complete opposite of the place they'd lived when his mother had been around. His mother was the one who was making more money, and his father was always between jobs. His momma worked as a teacher at the school Jacob currently attended. She left the job and Jacob just before he'd entered the seventh-grade class she taught. She loved every student that walked the halls of the school. When Jacob was in the sixth grade, the seventh-grade students would come up to him and tell him how cool she was, but he didn't know if they were being facetious. Near the end of the school year last year, a student said she allowed him to do an extra-credit project that helped him move on to the eighth grade. But Jacob knew all this already. Before she left him alone with an abusive father, she was the most loving mother and person anyone could ask for.

Jacob wandered through the graffiti-filled walls, the abandoned gas stations, and the homeless people who smelled of piss. Jacob's mother had always said to never wander the neighborhood on his own, but right now, he had no choice. Even if Bernie had woken, he looked to be in no condition to operate a motor vehicle.

Straight ahead after walking down the front steps of his father's home was the start of Prybrook Avenue. Prybrook was the worst street in the city of Greenville. It was home to ten of the thirteen homicides that occurred in the state last year. The street ran through the heart of the city and was twenty-one miles long. It held restaurants, top businesses, and the middle school Jacob attended. He was aware of the badness this street held, but if he took the long way around, he would not be able to submit his comic. So he needed to be brave like Captain Ember and defend the sun. In this case, the sun was himself.

He had done this walk three times before when his father wouldn't wake from a night out. Walking down here during the day with the sunshine painting the blacktop was much more comforting than walking through here at night.

Jacob had done this walk in the darkness once when he stayed after school for the Comic Book Club. This club had three students in it. The yearbook photo was a lonely one. Alex was in the club, along with this kid Leo. Alex couldn't make it that night, so it was Jacob, Leo, and Mr. Madsen who the school paid extra to watch over them sitting in silence, reading comics.

His mom had parent-teacher conferences that ran late into the night, and it was planned for his father to pick him up. Not surprisingly, he had never showed up. Jacob searched the hallways after his club, but it seemed his mother had left already. Jacob ran the entire way to his parents' home without stopping or looking anywhere other than straight ahead.

When he got there his father was sitting around the kitchen table drinking beer with three of his friends playing dominoes.

"Oh, hey bud, you look outta breath," he had said with a hearty laugh. He had gotten home in eight minutes, which was a record, since his old home was about a ten-minute drive from the school. His new home was a five-minute drive, but going up Prybrook felt long enough.

This time around Jacob was having an easier time strolling down the dangerous street. He placed his headphones over his ears and had the ten songs he'd downloaded onto his iPod Touch blaring into his eardrums.

He was in a Luther Vandross mood today. Luther's soulful voice sang to him. He even closed his eyes to try to remember his mom and him listening to this on her old record player. It spun around on its needle as his mother embraced him.

When Jacob opened his eyes, he was shocked to see a man standing on the solid yellow double line. He pulled his headphones down around his neck.

"Excuse me, little man."

Jacob stared blankly at a man with a long beard that was patchy in places. It looked as though he had alopecia on his face. The man smiled, multiple teeth missing, including the two in the front.

"Young man, can you spare some change?" the man said with a southern drawl.

The man was white, which was odd to see in this neighborhood. At first glance, he looked like he had darker skin, but as he got closer, he could see he was just dirty. His clothing—if you could call it that—was tattered and ripped. He wore a button-down shirt that was ripped exposing his dirty nipple. At the bottom it was stretched out, and the buttons were buttoned unevenly. His pants were in the same condition, but they sold jeans pre-ripped now, Jacob thought.

He stared at the man for a long few seconds, almost as if he didn't understand a word he said. The man's breath smelled of onions and urine, and Jacob felt a burning vomit build in his throat. He swallowed it back down.

Jacob shook his head in a surety of negativity and flipped the headphones back onto his head walking faster now toward the school. Jacob used his index finger to press the up volume on the side of his iPod to its highest setting, but it couldn't get any louder.

He could still hear the man behind him, yelling, "Hey!" and his footfalls getting closer. Jacob moved his legs to a full sprint now. Jacob peered over his shoulder to see the man running. It was more like a limp. The man looked to be galloping like a horse. He was making a noise with his mouth, a gurgling noise like his father did when brushing his teeth.

It reminded Jacob of a zombie from *The Walking Dead* TV show. Alex had shown him a clip of the show to show him how cool it was, but Jacob only excused himself to vomit his breakfast into the toilet in the school bathroom. He had that same feeling right now.

Jacob could see the front of the school in the distance, but the man was gaining on him. The man seemed to have speed on his gallop. The man reached Jacob and grabbed the top handle of his book bag with his bony hand that looked as though it lacked skin. Jacob was sure he seen his bone.

Jacob was yanked backward and onto the floor. He looked up at the leper-looking creature.

"Your personal choices affect the ones around you. Remember that."

Jacob crawled backward using his hands and feet like a crab staring at the man.

"Please, I don't know what you're talking about," Jacob said, reaching the steps of the school. He turned around and ran up the stairs, not looking back, almost falling, climbing up the cement staircase. Now he was inside safe. Sort of.

Chapter 8

2014

Jacob ran inside the home, with Alex tailing behind. Jacob's mother was resting on the couch with her feet on the glass coffee table, reading a magazine.

"Mom, can me and Alex go up to my room so I can show him my comic books?" Jacob said with excitement.

"*May Alex and I.*" Brenda corrected him. "And, yes of course, you can."

"Thank you, Mrs. Simeon, and it's nice to see you again," Alex said, politely holding his hands in front of him by his waist.

"If you don't call me Brenda, I'm gonna need to have a talk with your momma," Brenda said with a smile and a wink.

Alex took a few worrisome steps backward and said, "Thank you, Brenda," and jetted upstairs behind Jacob.

They reached his room, and Jacob immediately took out a brown cardboard box that he was hidden in his closet behind a pile of clothes. He picked up the flaps and pulled out each one, telling Alex who it was and what the story was about.

"This is Captain America; you probably know him already." He placed that one on the ground and took the next one out of the box. "And this is Green Lantern." Jacob showed Alex the cover.

"I thought Green Lantern was white," Alex said.

"There's a white guy named Hal Jordan and a black guy named John Stewart. I really want the one they both appear in. But John is my favorite." Jacob went to pull out another one.

"Your mom is nice," Alex said out of nowhere.

Jacob paused with a Batman comic in hand. "Oh, yeah she is. This one is—"

"Then why was your dad mean to her?" Alex asked, cutting him off.

Jacob paused, unsure of what to say. Jacob shrugged. "He just gets mad sometimes. My mom says it's because he drinks a lot of alcohol. But he's not a bad guy."

"It seems like he is a bad guy. If my dad hit me, I probably wouldn't ever talk to him again."

"You don't even know my dad," Jacob snapped. "He made bad mistakes like anybody else. Your parents aren't even around."

Alex slumped his shoulders and began walking to the door. "At least he calls me every day on the phone, and I can see him on video chat. I'm not going to say anything else bad about your dad. I'm sorry if I hurt your feelings, but you should know. That's something my dad taught me.

Never lay a hand on anyone unless your life depends on it. I think I'm gonna go."

Alex turned the door handle.

"I'm sorry, Alex," Jacob said.

"It's fine. I'll see you tomorrow," Alex said not looking back.

Jacob watched him leave from the top of the stairs. "Heading out so early Alex?" he heard Brenda ask.

"Dinnertime. Good night, Brenda." He watched Alex exit the front door.

Chapter 9

2019

Principal Owens greeted Jacob at the front entrance. He was a very tall man with broad shoulders with biceps like beer kegs, a scary figure to walk into, especially when you are late.

"Mr. Simeon, step into my office please." Jacob slumped his head with his chin on his collarbone and followed Principal Owens to his office down the hallway.

"Take a seat, please," Owens said in a somber tone.

Jacob threw his book bag onto the floor and bounced onto the comfy chair in front of Owens's desk. Owens sat in his own chair facing Jacob, looking fierce.

"Jacob, this is the fifth time this month you have been late. Now I don't enjoy disciplining my students, especially a star student such as yourself. Is there any reason you have been tardy so often?" Principal Owens sat back, and his chair creaked so loudly Jacob winced a bit.

Jacob sat back in the comfy chair also and thought. *Yes, either my dad fails to wake from nights he goes out drinking and God knows what. Or he wakes up telling me he is going to take me, and then he falls back asleep, and I need to go through the long process of waking the Frankenstein that is my own father. Oh, and my reluctance to come to a school where I am bullied daily, but you and the rest of your teachers just look the other way. It's even a wonder I'm still showing up here.*

"No, no reason," Jacob said clearing his throat.

"Because you know you can talk to me about anything, whether it be something that happens here or at home. You know that, don't you, son?" Principal Owens clasped his fingers together and placed them on his lap waiting on a response.

I had come to you before when I was lying in the middle of the hallway after Robbie Stan shoved me into a locker, with blood trickling down both nostrils into my mouth. You said you would 'look into' the situation. And as for my home situation—

Principal Owens tapped an unsharpened pencil on his desk impatiently.

"Yes, sir, I know," Jacob pushed out through his lips.

"Okay, I will let you off with a warning today, but one more time and I will be forced to take disciplinary action. Now get to class."

Jacob rose slowly and exited the office.

When Jacob arrived at Mrs. Donaldson's algebra class, she was in the middle of drawing a triangle on the blackboard with numbers at two sides side along with an X. The silent class to her back were scribbling in their notebooks. She flipped her wrist to her face to look at her small watch. "Class begins at 8:00 a.m., Mr. Simeon."

Jacob stood frozen at the front of the classroom with fifteen pairs of eyes on him. He stared at the green linoleum floor and took his seat next to his best friend.

"Do you have it?" Alex whispered with excitement.

Jacob said nothing but reached into his book bag and pulled out his comic book creation. Alex grabbed it out of Jacob's hand.

"Hey!" Jacob said playfully and softly.

Alex flipped through the pages quickly and reached to the final page. Alex held it up in Jacob's direction and said: "What's good with this?"

"Didn't have time." Jacob said with a frown forming on his lips. "But I can finish it this period.".

"Gentleman, do you mind?" Mrs. Donaldson's voice flew from the front of the classroom.

"Sorry, miss, continue please." Alex said with a sarcastic tone.

Mrs. Donaldson, who the kids called Mrs. Donald Duck due to her squeaky voice, rolled her eyes and continued with the lesson.

"Are you sure you can finish it with Donald Duck teaching?" Alex spoke in a whisper. Jacob peered at Alex and nodded. Jacob did not enjoy getting in trouble, but the problem with Alex is he was born to be in trouble.

Jacob moved his large Algebra I book to the right revealing the unfinished page. Jacob slid the twenty-four-color pencil set from his book bag and slowly began to shade his drawing. Then the bell rang.

"Fuck," Jacob muttered.

Jacob and Alex strolled toward the cafeteria.

"What am I going to do, Alex? This is due right now, and it's incomplete." Jacob was shaking and his breaths were becoming sharper by the second.

Alex attempted to comfort him. "Dude, it's an amazing comic. I don't think they will mind if a page is not colored."

"No, they take points off for unfinished sections." Jacob had a tear fall down his cheek.

Alex nodded his head and walked forward.

"Alex, where are you going?"

Alex looked back at him and placed his hand out in front of him. Basically saying "he got this." Jacob followed close behind his friend as he approached the table in the hallway outside the cafeteria. The paper sign hanging on the front read GREENVILLE COMIC COMPETITION. It was on a purple poster board with various superheroes pasted around the text, which looked to be taken from Google images.

"Excuse me, sir," Alex said to a teacher, Mr. Henderson, who sat behind the wooden table. "My friend did not have a chance to finish coloring one page. Is there any way you can cut him a break?”

Jacob backed away as both the teacher, and Alex stared at him.

“The comics are not due until the end of the lunch period, so there is still time,” the teacher explained with a friendly smile.

Jacob looked up, overjoyed, when Mr. Henderson finished speaking. “Come on, Alex. That gives me enough time.” Jacob tugged Alex’s arm and skipped into the cafeteria.

Jacob was beaming as he colored his final page. The tables in the cafeteria were splintered and had dents from years of children using them. They were not the best conditions for drawing, but he didn’t have a choice, and it would need to do.

“You’re gonna win my dude,” Alex said sitting directly next to him on the table with benches on both sides.

“So, who are you taking to the convention anyway?” Alex asked, but Jacob was frantically shading ignoring his friend’s question. “Jacob,” Alex whispered frantically into his ear.

Jacob jumped, but did not go outside the lines. “I don’t know, Alex. I might not even go. What I want more is my work hung in the hallway for all the students to—” Jacob stopped without looking up.

"Oh shit," Alex said, tapping Jacob on the shoulder.

"Whatever it is, it can wait," Jacob said, still not looking up. Then the papers were pulled from the table and on to the floor of the cafeteria. They floated down in almost slow motion as Jacob looked on in horror. All the students that were eating seconds ago stopped and stared at Alex, Jacob, and Robbie Stan. Robbie stood at the end of the table, grinning and proud of what he had just done.

"Drawing your little comics, you nerds," Robbie said as he watched Jacob on his hands and knees collecting his work.

Robbie picked up the cover page of the comic. "Captain Ember!" Robbie roared into laughter. "What a load of shit."

Robbie snagged one of the pages and held it to his lips and blew on the edge, imitating a ripping sound. Jacob sat there in silence with a look of concern over his face.

"Give it to him, asshole." Alex was standing now and yelling behind Jacob.

"Oh, you mean this? Well, if you can reach it, you can have it." Robbie held the paper above Jacob's head, pulling it up each time Jacob tried to reach out for it.

Alex stepped up on the seating bench and then the table and jumped, grabbed the paper from Robbie's hand and gave it to Jacob. Robbie cackled and walked away like a schoolgirl. Jacob put his head back down and concentrated on his coloring as Alex collected the others papers from the floor.

"I'm gonna finish in time, Alex," Jacob said with the most joy Alex had ever heard from him, and he smiled too.

"Heads up." Jacob and Alex heard from behind them. A small, square metal box with a small red flame flew above their heads and onto the table. Red and orange flames engulfed the comic as though there was gasoline poured beforehand. The whole comic Jacob had worked on for months, ever since the competition was announced, evaporating before his eyes in seconds.

It was a black hole in his world quickly sucked out his life. Alex came rushing with a cup of water and splashed it onto the table. The flames went out, and the pages of comics had a black-rimmed hole in the center. Jacob could not move; he could not say anything. His mouth hung open, but nothing could escape from it. Jacob turned to see Robbie on the floor holding his gut laughing.

Alex appeared in Jacob's line of sight as he watched Robbie stand up and wipe the tears from his eyes. A punch was thrown. Robbie was clocked in the face and stumbled, falling back to the linoleum floor. The other students in the cafeteria let out a collective gasp. Robbie's smile was wiped from his face, and he attempted a strike back, but his swing was caught by Mr. Henderson.

"Both of you, Principal Owens's office now!" Mr. Henderson yelled.

The other students had stopped their chewing and small chatter, and all eyes were on Alex and Robbie. They both went toward the office with Robbie leading the way since he was there nearly every day. Mr. Henderson approached Jacob, who had tears streaming.

"Are you okay, son?" Jacob made a squeaking sound because that was all he could manage to get out. The teacher picked up the blackened shreds of paper that lay on the table.

"Unfortunately, I can't accept this. I'm sorry," he said. Jacob didn't have a response; he ran out of the cafeteria. The other kids with their eyes on him like a cat following a mouse.

Chapter 10

2015

Bernie sat on the couch with his feet on the glass table, flipping through the channels. He threw back a beer and crushed it with his hand and tossed it on the same table where five more crushed cans laid in a pile. Jacob waddled into the front door through the living room with his sights set on locking himself in his room.

"Hey, come over here, son," he said, waving his hand.

Jacob continued as though he hadn't heard him.

"I know you heard me, boy. Now get your ass over here." He slammed his hand hard on the spot on the couch next to him.

Jacob slid his feet across the floor and pulled himself onto the couch.

"How is school going?" he asked, pulling another beer from the floor to his left.

Jacob shrugged his shoulders and said, "Just started." His voice came out raspy and sounded as though he hadn't spoken in years.

"Any girls at school that you like?" he said, moving his eyebrows up and down and nudging him in the shoulder. Jacob's gaze was fixed on the hardwood floor and moved his head from left to right breathing out a soft "No."

Jacob jumped as his father slammed a hand down next to him.

"Speak up. boy," Bernie yelled at him.

"Jacob, baby, can you come in here, please." Jacob felt relief wash over him at the sound of his mother's voice. He slid off the couch and jogged through the door that led into the kitchen.

Brenda was standing in front of the stove where a breaded chicken breast was sizzling on a black skillet. She was wearing a blue denim dress that fell to her knees. But a smile was her best feature, and she was wearing a big one. She had her hands behind her back.

"I got you something," she said excitedly. She brought a rectangle wrapped package to her front and handed it to him. He tore through the purple wrapping paper to reveal Hal Jordan on the ground being held up by John Stewart both in their Green Lantern uniforms.

Jacob recognized it right away from the pictures he had seen of it online. Jacob collapsed to the floor, hugging it in his arms and crying. His mother lifted him and placed the book on the kitchen table, and they embraced each other.

"Thank you so, so much," Jacob said in a clear voice now through his sobs.

"Okay, don't let your father see that comic or that you're crying. Bring it up to your room and hide it."

Jacob shot a look of concern at his mother.

"I'll distract him." Even though his father would be facing the TV with his back to the stairs Jacob was concerned Bernie would spot him. Jacob nodded, and Brenda sat next to Bernie. Jacob tiptoed past his kissing parents and up the stairs.

"Was that Jacob?" Bernie said, pulling away from her lips.

"Yeah, don't worry about him. Worry about me." She pulled him in again, and they made out for a few minutes.

"The fuck was that about. You haven't kissed me like that, or at all, in years," he noted, pulling an unopened beer from beside him.

"So I can have your full attention. Do you remember when I let you move back in?"

Bernie nodded, confused.

"And I told you to stop drinking." She pulled the beer from his closed hand. "And told you to get a job." She placed the full beer on the table in front of them.

"And I have applied every day. I can't just, poof, have a job appear in front of me," he said, waving his hands in her face. She forced his hands out of her face. "I have a job for you. It's not a high-paying job, but it's something."

He gave a her a grin and said, "What?"

"It's called cleaning up after yourself."

She stood and went to the kitchen, coming back with a garbage bag. She tossed the bag onto his lap.

"It's so easy even you can do it," she said, making her way up the stairs.

She could hear the footfalls of her husband behind her and felt her curled crochet braids get tugged back. She whipped her head around and lunged forward landing the crown of her head up under his jaw. A cracking sound followed by a scream—a girly scream—left her husband's mouth. He lost his balance and fell backward, tumbling over the back of the couch and through the glass table. She gave a smirk and headed up the stairs. At the top was Jacob crying, and he bolted into his room, slamming the door.

Brenda was lightly tapping on Jacob's bedroom door for a few minutes now.

"Jacob, honey, can we talk about this, please?" She pressed the side of her face to the door, but all she could hear were muffled sobs. She turned around and slid her back down the same door, her butt hitting the floor and her knees to her chest.

"Do you remember when we watched the Spider-Man movie?" She listened for a response, but there was only silence. "And he was fighting the bully, Frank or something."

"Flash," she heard from the room, and her mouth curled up into a smile.

"Right, and Flash was picking on him all the time, and when he couldn't control his web, he accidently hit him in the head," she said and listened. There was nothing, but she assumed he was listening. "He was ducking and dodging all those punches and finished with a punch of his own? You remember, right?"

An inaudible noise that sounded like a "Yeah" came through the white wooden door, which was thinner than the door Bernie had kicked down. It was the cheapest option at the time.

"So, while it's not okay to hit anybody, when someone is attacking you, you should defend yourself." Small footfalls pattered across the floor, and the door opened.

Brenda almost fell into his room at his feet. Jacob plopped down and sat cross-legged, staring at his mother.

"Why does Dad hurt you and me? Because you taught me to not hit people. Even Alex asked me a few months ago. And don't say it's because he drinks a lot," Jacob said in a strong voice.

Brenda focused her vision on the ground in front of her. "He is not a nice person, Jacob," she said, not looking at him.

"Then why after he hit you, you let him live with us again?"

Brenda was shocked at the maturity of the question. It was a good question that she didn't really know the answer to. "It's late, you should get to bed," she said, hearing the sprinkling of glass from below.

"No, I want an answer. Because if he's still sleeping one room away, I want to know he won't hurt you or me."

She pulled herself to her feet, and so did Jacob.

"Because he said he'd changed, and I believed him. But after what happened downstairs—" She paused, choking back tears. "He's gone for good."

They embraced each other.

"Hang on, Mom, I got something for you." He ran to his bedside drawer and pulled out a small box and hid it behind his back. He looked up at her and smiled, showing her the small velvet box.

Brenda took the beige box and flipped it open to reveal a gold necklace. Hanging on the chain was a round locket. She undid the latch and opened it up. Inside was a picture Jacob that she had taken while at the park one day. She had to squint to read what it said in the middle.

"It says, 'I love you forever.'" Jacob was holding his hands close to his chest. Brenda was crying the tears she had been holding back from the fight, and knelt hugging her son.

"I love you more." She walked off holding the necklace in her palm and close to her heart. She looked back, and she was so happy to see him smiling.

Chapter 11

2019

Jacob wasn't going back to class; he couldn't. That comic was all he had to look forward to. He had pictured winning and the students and teachers giving him a loud, roaring round of applause. He had pictured going home and telling his father he had done something great. Not that his dad would care much.

But it was all gone in mere seconds. All the work he had done had disintegrated right in front of his eyes. Jacob exited the front doors of school and began the slow walk back to his shithole home

"Jacob, wait up, man." Alex jogged up behind him.

Jacob grabbed his hand with a firm shake. "Thank you," Jacob said and grabbed him around his neck, bringing him in close for a hug. Alex patted him on his back, and then Jacob released him from his hold.

"What did they give you?" Jacob asked.

"Suspension for the rest of the day," Alex said as he shrugged his shoulders. "It's cool. I could use a day off." Alex was so calm and collected. That is one of the things Jacob loved about his best friend.

"What about the other guy?" Jacob asked, still walking slowly down Prybrook with Alex right beside him.

"Not sure what his punishment was, but he's got one hell of a bruise," Alex said with enthusiasm.

"You got him real good," Jacob said, attempting to form a smile.

"Hey, let's go to our spot," Alex said, running ahead, waving for Jacob to follow.

***

Alex bent back a piece of a broken chain-link fence and hurried Jacob through. Alex slid through after. They approached the old abandoned factory with broken windows, brick laid to the top, and a roof luckily still intact.

Alex tore the large piece of plywood from the open doorway. They rushed inside, and Alex maneuvered the plywood back in the doorway. Jacob paused before he stepped inside, flashing back to the incident with Robbie where he'd got pushed into the railing on the outside after a chase on the inside.

Empty black conveyor belts snaked through the large open space. They walked to one of the offices that were lined against the walls. Alex opened the desk drawer and reached inside. Jacob shuttered. When Alex's hand came up, he was holding two brown rectangle boxes with M&M's printed on the side.

"I know they're your favorite," Alex said, and Jacob felt a rush of heat cover take over his face. He tossed one at Jacob, and Jacob caught it at the last second. "I stashed some here the other day."

Jacob's smile remained as they tore their boxes of candy open. They sat in the two rolling chairs and talked for hours about school, the fight that had happened, and how it was okay that Jacob didn't win the comic competition. Jacob felt relieved and much better, thanks to his best friend.

It was getting close to full dark now, and Jacob noticed the streetlamps coming to life. He hadn't realized truly how long they had been talking.

"I should probably get home before my dad has a fit," Jacob said somberly. Alex was now sitting on top of the desk facing Jacob, who was still in the office chair. Jacob looked at Alex and smiled the biggest grin he had ever done before.

"What? Do I have chocolate in my teeth?" Alex said, scratching his tooth with his fingernail.

"I'm just glad we're friends," Jacob said, still grinning ear to ear.

"I am too. You're a good dude," Alex said as he slid off the desk.

"I mean that, like, nobody has ever stood up for me like you did. It means everything," Jacob said as he rose to his feet.

"Yeah, man, nobody fucks with my buddy," Alex said with a smile of his own. They stood in the office for another long few seconds, staring at each other—Jacob with the endless grin and Alex looking confused, with his eyebrows arched.

Jacob's sweat was dripping off his chin. Then he closed his eyes and leaned in with his lips pursed. Jacob could smell Alex's cologne and the soap he'd used this morning. Then a hand, a strong hand, pushed his face away. Jacob lost his balance and fell to the ground. His head bounced like a basketball off the concrete floor where a piece of the carpeting had been removed.

Jacob woke minutes later with Alex standing over him. "Are you all right, man?"

Jacob fluttered his eyes to stop the blurriness. "What happened?" Jacob said, holding the back of his head.

"Um, I think you tried to kiss me. Then you fell back and hit your head," Alex said, offering his hand.

Jacob took it and rose to his feet. He was a bit wobbly when he got up but caught his balance.

"So, I'm gonna take off. Um, catch you later," Alex said, turning to leave and awkwardly pointing at the exit.

"Wait!" Jacob yelled, probably too loudly as his voice echoed off the walls.

Alex turned and looked at Jacob with his head sideways and lips moving. Jacob could tell that he is upset, but spoke anyway: "We're still cool right?"

Alex did a small eye roll and responded. "Yeah, man, we cool."

"Because it seems like you're upset with me," Jacob said with hopeful eyes.

"It's cool, man. I just don't roll that way," Alex said in a hushed tone.

"Oh…I mean, yeah…me either. I was just…" Jacob paused and found it difficult to speak anymore.

Alex walked away and into the darkness of the factory. Alex kicked the plywood down and left it laying in the grassy area just outside. Jacob was left standing in the office alone. The way he always felt.

Jacob watched his friend walk away from him and couldn't move. He stood there next to the factory belts, crying, thinking about who he had remaining in his life.

None of the teachers at school cared about him, his father barely noticed he was around, his mother left him who is probably with a new guy living a new life, and now his best friend would most likely never speak to him again.

Jacob stepped over the plywood makeshift door that had cut in half. It reminded him of his father kicking in the door to his bedroom a few years back.

***

It took Jacob longer than usual to get home, but he made it inside. As he walked through the kitchen, he caught a glimpse of something in his peripheral vision. It was a white piece of paper torn into an uneven triangle with tear marks along the sides. Jacob picked it up and saw it had a handwritten note on the front, but he immediately turned it over, curious what it had been written on the back of. It was a notice from the bank about foreclosure on the house due to lack of payments. It was dated three months ago. Jacob was fighting through his eyelids between the tears he had built up on his walk home. He read the note:

> *Hey bud,*
>
> *I'm gonna head out and get some milk should be back by supper. There is a frozen TV dinner thing in the freezer if you want it.*
>
> *DAD*

Jacob crumpled the paper into a ball and threw it at the wall, and it softly fell to the floor. Jacob let out a loud crying roar and collapsed to the floor. His eyes went to the dark outside, and all he could hear were the chirp of crickets. There were no cars whirring by. There were no gunshots, which was a common sound in this part of the city. There weren't even the homeless people yelling at each other. It was Jacob and only Jacob.

He climbed from the floor and rushed to the refrigerator. Hung by a magnet was Aunt Carrie's number. He used the landline phone that hung next to the fridge and punched her number in. It rang four times, and Jacob thought she wouldn't pick up.

"Hello? Bernie is that you? I told you I never wanted to speak to you ever again. Hello? Do you hear me?" she said.

Jacob's sobs were so bad he couldn't get a word out.

"I'm busy. Call me later," she said in a haste.

The line went dead.

With him knowing his father was never coming back home. Not just because it was late at night and he wasn't here, or because of the note, but because he knew in his heart that his father never cared about him, he only ever cared about himself and whatever bottle he was carrying. And even if he did return, why would he want a gay, loser son to care for?

Jacob opened the squeaking door to his father's room, which he was never allowed to step foot into.

He had been in here a few times to wake his father to drive him to school, only to take knuckles to the jaw. He sat at the desk that sat at the foot of his father's bed and powered up the computer, the one his father said to "never even lay a finger on."

He wasn't sure if he could get far enough since the water from his eyes were falling between the letters on the keyboard. He was so frustrated that while he it was booting up, he picked up the keyboard and smashed it against the table.

Keys *P*, *D*, and *J* flew out and one struck him in the middle of his big forehead. He noticed a small shiny object hanging out from underneath the board. He picked up a gold chain, and at the end hung a locket with the picture of him and his mother, the very one he'd gifted to her.

Jacob held it close to his heart and placed it around his neck. In the glow of the screen, the streams of dried tears on his cheeks illuminated. He clicked open the internet browser and used the search field to type: "How to tie a noose."

Chapter 12

2018

Bernie had graduated from beer cans to large liquor bottles. Tonight was the three liter of Jack Daniel's whiskey he purchased earlier in the morning. He had been the only one standing outside the store waiting for the owner to flip the sign from closed to open.

Now the clock had just struck midnight, and he was three-fourths through. His soon-to-be ex-wife and son were in their deep slumbers upstairs. Bernie, however, was in the unfinished basement, sitting on the cold cement ground. The glow of his smart phone was the only light illuminating his face. The bing-bong sounds from the game he was playing echoed throughout the room.

Then came the sound of a text tone and the clicks of his keyboard. Bernie released a maniacal laugh and got up from his cross-legged position. He went to the rectangle basement window, and a woman appeared outside. From Bernie's view, you could see up her short skirt as she crouched. She was white, with a scary-skinny figure and you could see the outline of her ribs.

Bernie tugged on the window, but it wouldn't budge. He held up his index finger to the woman to indicate to her to wait a second. He took a red brick from the pile when he had the urge to build a fireplace at one time. He tossed it at the window without warning, and it exploded in the woman's face in a loud crash.

Upstairs, Brenda was lying in her bed with her eyes wide open, staring at the bedside clock that had shown its switch to midnight.

A new day, she thought. Her father always used to say when you've had a bad day or if you were in a bad mood, it was refreshing to see the clock strike midnight. It meant everything was in the past now—a new day to make new better memories. When she was a little girl, there had been an old grandfather clock that belonged to her great-great-grandfather that would ring twelve times at midnight, and she would be able fall straight asleep. Brenda wished she had that clock right now.

Instead of twelve bongs, she heard a faint crash of glass breaking. She sat up quickly and threw the covers off. It was a humid night, but she kept her room cool. She knew Bernie was downstairs, so she figured he just drunkenly dropped a glass or a full bottle. She didn't care too much if he was hurt, but she figured she should at least check on him. The divorce was being finalized tomorrow, and that was when she would finally build enough courage to kick him out of her house for good.

Bernie pulled the woman through the small window. It wasn't a tight squeeze, but the seven-foot drop wasn't pleasant for her fragile body. Bernie couldn't stop giggling as she peeled herself off the hard ground.

"You got the stuff?" Bernie said with a hiccup.

She sat up on her nonexistent butt and feet flat on the ground swinging the small purse she was carrying. She opened it and brought out a glass pipe that had a skinny mouthpiece attached to a round glass ball with black residue stuck on.

The small woman removed a baggie and poured the contents into the pipe. Bernie had his own zippo lighter and flicked the flame to the bowl and breathed in the smoke and released it.

"Let me have some." The woman spoke for the first time, and her voice was deep and raspy.

Bernie pulled away. "I paid for the whole fucking thing and that's what I get." Bernie took another drag and released it with a satisfied moan.

"Actually, you haven't paid yet, so you shouldn't even be taking any of it at all," she said.

She pulled at Bernie's large forearm, and it wasn't moving an inch. She was now hanging as Bernie placed the pipe on his lips again. He blew the smoke into her face, but it didn't seem to bother her. Bernie then swung her around in circles. Something he used to do with Jacob. Her legs were dangling, and their forearms were interlocked. Then he unclasped his arms, and she landed on her legs. Her right one snapped like a twig, bending in the wrong direction. She collapsed and her head bounced off the concrete. Blood pooled underneath her, and she wasn't moving. Bernie peered down to notice the pipe wasn't in his hand anymore. It was by his feet broken in two pieces.

He was so flushed with anger he grabbed the only other thing in the basement, the liquor bottle.

He stood over the dead woman and smashed the bottle across her skull. New lacerations formed on her cheeks and lip, but she remained unmoved. He turned the bottle to the sharp shards that remained of the bottle and forced it straight down. The neck of the bottle stuck in her temple. Bernie was breathing heavy and turned to head upstairs, but that was where his wife stood with her hand over her mouth and eyes wide.

"No, no, no, no, no, it's not what it looks like—this wasn't my fault—I didn't do that," he stuttered, pointing at what remained.

When he turned back, she was halfway up the stairs. He started after her, but he stumbled at the bottom step. Then she closed the door and locked him down there.

Brenda hurried to her purse sitting on the kitchen counter. She dumped the contents onto the countertop, including makeup, keys, and tampons. The booming sound behind her made her jump. Bernie was yelling as he ran his foot into the door. Then after a few more, it stopped.

She ran her hand through the items quickly.

"Where is it? Fuck," She muttered to herself. Her hands were shaking as she threw the purse to the side in anger. She rushed upstairs and opened the door to Jacob's room. She saw a lump on his bed with a light filling the makeshift fort. There was no movement as she pulled the thin sheet off. Jacob fell backward and yelled. The flashlight he was holding momentarily blinded her as it dropped off the bed.

Jacob pulled his over-the-ear headphones off. A comic book sat opened on his pillow he was using as a stand.

"What…what happened?" Jacob asked after his breathing had calmed. Brenda stood, stunned, not sure of what to say.

"Do you…have you seen my cell phone?" she asked. He could take it and play the games, but only with her permission. He moved his head slowly from left to right, his eyes bulging from his sockets.

"Okay, look, I have to go. Some-somethings going on, and I will be right back, okay?" she collected herself and began to head for the door.

"Why?" Jacob's voice was grainy and made her jump again. She went to him, now kneeling where he slept, and she hugged him. When she let go, Jacob's attention went to the gold necklace he had gotten her months ago. He smiled, seeing her still wearing it. She reached her fingers behind her neck and unclasped it. She held the shimmering chain and locket in front of him. His brows furrowed, and the lines in his forehead became more apparent.

"I want you to have it," she said.

"Why?" It was the kind of question children ask in response to everything.

Her hand was really shaking now, she noticed. "Because I don't know that I can take care of it the way you want me to." The tears were apparent on her cheeks now.

"No, I gave it to you. It's my good luck charm to you. Now tell me what's going on."

She placed the necklace back around her neck and hurried out of the room without an answer.

Brenda collected all the items and shoved them back into her purse except for her car keys. She slung the large brown Michael Kors bag over her shoulder and exited the front door.

The front porch light wasn't lit, but she had no time to worry about that. She jangled her keys when she found the fob for her sedan. She honked it unlocked, and the headlights and rear lights flashed. The pain in the right side of her face came in the seconds after she hit the unlock button.

The taste of grass and the hard ground surrounded her swirling world now. Large hands wrapped around her legs, and now looking at the shiny sparks in the dark sky, she was traveling to the side of her home. Her head was swimming, but when she recognized her husband standing over her with a baseball bat, she knew this was very real.

He came down with the wooden home run–hitting instrument. She used her remaining strength to roll to the right side. When the impact of the bat hit the ground, she turned and saw his open legs as an opening. She threw her leg up into his groin area, expecting him to writhe in pain and fall to the floor. But he remained standing with a grin shaping his face.

"Oh yeah. Ouch," he said with a hearty laugh to follow. He lifted the bat again.

"Wait," she said with her arm outstretched and knees to her chest. "Look, why don't we go inside and talk about this? What happened in the basement didn't happen at all. I promise I won't say anything. You can even have the house and Jacob." She immediately regretted saying that last part.

He placed the top of the bat in the dirt, and she could see him calming down.

"We could even, you know." She ran her skinny fingers up from her crotch and cupped her small breasts.

He laughed again. "Oh, I'm gonna get mines. You just won't remember it." He raised the bat one more time, but he didn't miss when it came down this time. Multiple times. Her face imploded, with blood splattering in the grass and on the fence between the neighbors and their homes.

"Mom? Mom, are you there?" The screen door slammed as Jacob walked out the front door. Bernie remained still in the darkness that surrounded the home. Jacob went to his mother's car and pressed his face against the window to peer inside.

As soon as he did that, Bernie was dragging the mutilated body to the backyard along with her purse and keys. He moved her to behind the shed that held the lawn mower and other gardening tools neither of them used. He went in the back door, taking his shirt and shoes off. The front door slammed again. It was Jacob back inside.

Bernie crept upstairs and started the shower. He brought his blood-stained clothes in with him. Jacob entered the bathroom just as he stepped in the tub, throwing the curtain in front of him.

"Yeah, buddy," he said in a concerned tone.

"Where's Mom? She looked worried when she talked to me just now. I can't find her or her stuff."

Bernie paused for a second and then responded, "Yeah, she just went to the store for milk. She'll be right back. Just go to bed and you'll see her in the morning."

Jacob gave an upbeat "Okay, thanks, Dad." And skipped off to his bedroom, closing the bathroom door.

Chapter 13

2019

Jacob swung the closet door open and entered. He found some brown tough rope with the rope hairs protruding everywhere. He tugged on it, and it didn't budge. He brought the rope to the computer and placed the brown snake on the table next to the monitor.

He looked at the computer screen and then the rope, then the screen, then the rope. Tying various loops as he went on. It reminded him of the time his father had forced him into manly activities such as Boy Scouts.

He remembered sitting at a splintered picnic table with five other boys and the scoutmaster. He was teaching them how to tie a square knot. Jacob would take the rope under when he needed to go through, and he was never able to get the correct tie.

But Jacob finished this one, and it looked to be the same as the one on the internet. He even tested it by holding the loop part and pulling on the top. It worked perfectly. He dragged the heavy wood table from the kitchen, where his father and he never ate dinner together, into his bedroom. He stood on the table and bounced up and down to check the sturdiness. The table was a bit wobbly, but he didn't care.

He then retrieved a ladder from the basement. He used it to tie the rope to the ceiling fan in his room. The fan didn't spin, and when he'd told his father, Bernie had only told him to fix it himself. He wasn't sure if it would hold, but he hoped it would crush his skull if it fell on top of him anyway. He tied it as tightly as he could and hung the noose down. It swayed back and forth on its own. Jacob wrapped his fingers around it and hung his body weight for a few seconds. He was chubby for his age, and he heard a bit of cracking coming from the fan, but it didn't deter him.

Jacob placed a foot up on the wobbly wood table and took a deep breath in and let it out. He paused and looked at his small comic book collection and his desk where he worked so many hours on his project.

He placed his foot back on the safe ground and sat at his desk, where he'd drawn out various versions of his favorite superheroes and villains. Now he could only think how much time he wasted on something that nobody would ever lay their eyes on. He ripped out a sheet of drawing paper from his pad and slammed it on his desk. He began to write:

Dear Whoever,

I'm writing this letter to let you know you won't be seeing me anymore. In my twelve years of living, it's been a shitshow. Between my family and school, I haven't lived the American dream. My only saving graces were my best friend Alex, who won't be friends with me anymore because he found out I am in love with him, as more than friends. I'm sorry, Alex. My mother was my number one. WAS. Until

Jacob pulled the tear-soaked paper from the top of his desk and stood on the chair, reading it aloud to the empty house. He released it, and it gently floated to the floor directly below the noose. He took out every drawing he ever spent hours of his day on while the other kids played outside and tore them to shreds. Pieces of his art, his short life's work.

Ever since he had been five years old, he'd wanted to draw and was in love with comic books. But that didn't matter now. What mattered now was moving on from the world and getting on with the next life. Jacob grabbed the box of matches from his dad's room and burned all his work in a metal trash can.

Jacob stepped onto the unsteady death stand. The table wobbled to the left and right of him slightly. He found his balance like trying to surf and grabbed the rope hanging from the ceiling fan. Jacob drew in a deep breath, held it for a few seconds, and slowly released it. He placed the noose around his throat. He'd learned on the internet that the rope doesn't choke you to death, but it breaks the top two vertebrae in your neck by the impact of the fall, which kills you instantly if done correctly. He couldn't mess this up, or he would be hanging there, struggling. He didn't want to struggle; he just wanted to relieve his mental pain as quickly as possible.

He was looking out his bedroom window and, from this height, could see the sidewalk across the street. The old homeless man from Prybrook Avenue stood there staring at him. He still had his dirty, ripped clothing on. Jacob wondered if he was already dead. And the words the man had said came floating back to his mind like an infection.

Your personal choices affect the one's around you. Remember that.

The man stood there and moved his head slowly from left to right. This made Jacob lose his balance, and the table fell on its side hitting the floor, but Jacob did not. The rope caught his neck and pulled. The rope creaked and the ceiling fan held up. He knew it would.

Jacob was still conscious. He'd messed up, he thought. The rope was choking him. Gurgling sounds emitted from his mouth. His arms and legs were fluttering around him. All he saw was the old man shaking his head in disapproval, that was all he could see. He was beginning to feel tired, and his breaths became further apart and shallower. His thinking became nonexistent. Then darkness overtook his mind.

Nothingness remained.

Nothing.

Part II

Jacob was falling. He didn't know where. But he was falling. His arms were flailing by his sides like windmills, and his legs were fluttering. All around him was darkness. Like being in the night sky with the absence of stars and the moon. He attempted to turn his body to see where he was falling. He wasn't losing any breath, which was surprising because walking up three stairs made him feel like he'd run a marathon.

When he got his body around, he saw a small square of white light. He always heard that when you die, you should stay away from the white light. Don't run toward it. That's where heaven is. But Jacob wanted to go there. Jacob believed he was a good person and always did the right thing, so he would go to heaven. And when he talked with God, God would tell him it's not his time, and God would send him back down to earth. But what Jacob really wanted was to be just like one of the superheroes he read about—to die and, through some miracle, gain superpowers and rid his city of crime and destroy his enemies.

As the square got closer and more visible, Jacob realized he didn't have a choice. He was going to this place whether he wanted to or not. Jacob pulled his knees to his chest and closed his eyes tightly, bracing for whatever impact may come.

The temperature was cold, and Jacob was in a Captain America T-Shirt and a pair of And1 black-and-red basketball shorts. While in the fetal position, he felt a temperature change. It was a comfortable environment, and he opened his eyes. He was curled up in his own bed. He was underneath his duvet like he had just woken up. Only there was no morning sunlight. It was like those days it would rain and be gloomy in the morning and he had a difficult time waking up. He turned and looked up at the ceiling fan—which was working now—and the brown rope noose was swaying from side to side still intact.

Jacob slowly crawled from under his covers and opened his bedroom door. It was just like the house where his father and he had lived, only it was dark and deserted. Scared, he walked back to his bed and got onto his knees, placing his hands together, interlocking his fingers, resting his forearms onto the flimsy mattress, closing his eyes.

"Dear God, I don't know what's happening, and I don't know why I'm not dead. Or am I dead? Is this heaven or hell? Please send me something and let me know. Amen." He prayed out loud and opened his eyes to his father's round belly. Jacob scurried backward and fell off the bed on his butt. His father rose from his bed and planted his feet on the ground and exited, the door slamming behind him.

The bright sunshine that painted the floor and walls of his room so many times before were not present, and darkness was spread throughout and outside. Jacob peered out the window next to his bed, but it was as though a black garbage bag had been placed over the outside. Jacob decided to follow where his father had gone and exited his room.

Outside the door was not the living room, it was a long hallway filled with identical wooden doors on either side. As he stepped into the hall, the door behind him shut on its own and locked. Jacob couldn't even turn the handle to go back in.

Jacob was feeling surprisingly calm for what was happening. He wandered down the desolate corridor, which seemed to be never-ending. He decided that he needed to just choose a door at random. It was like the Memory Game he'd played with his mom. His mother would use two decks of playing cards and pick out duplicates, one from each deck. She would show them to Jacob and then flip them, over and he had to remember where the two duplicates were. Jacob would forget every time and begin to guess on every turn. But right now, he had no idea what was behind these brown doors.

He picked one, the one directly in front of him at random. He turned the handle, and inside was an exact replica of the hallway he just left. The endless row of doors again was all he could see.

He began selecting doors until he saw something different than this corridor of doors. He ran down this current hallway feeling his flabby stomach and arms bouncing as he opened doors. He peered behind each door to see what was inside.

He reached a right-side door, and he noticed something immediately different. There was thick, dark smoke billowing from the inside. He stopped running, not out of breath at all. He stepped through the door, choking a bit, and his eyes burned, but he chose to ignore that. It was indeed another hallway, but this one he recognized. This one he knew very well. It was the hallway at his school.

Chapter 15

Greenville Middle School was dark but the light from the fires lit the way. The emergency lights were also on which went on when there was a blackout or a fire. From the smell and vision, he thought the latter. The school no longer looked like a school or any building. The roof had large holes in random places as though it was in the path of a meteor shower. All the windows that provided the sunlight that Jacob enjoyed feeling on his face during class, especially when it was nearing summer vacation, were blown out. The shards of glass sprinkled on the outside.

The double doors in the front were hanging on by the bottom hinges. Jacob walked on the green linoleum tiles that carried him past the blue lockers and the open classroom doors.

He entered the first classroom on the right. He flashed back to Mrs. Donaldson mocking him every time he was late for class. When was he going to use algebra in his lifetime anyway? Jacob thought and jumped, releasing a small squeak when the classroom door shut on its own. Jacob attempted to turn the handle, but it wouldn't budge. He threw his heavy body into the door, but he only came up with a hurt shoulder. The white socks that came halfway up his calves were painted with thick black dust. He stared longingly into the empty hallway of billowing smoke through the rectangle window just above the metal handle.

Jacob slammed his back on the door and slid down to the floor. He placed his hands through his small dark afro in frustration. Looking down at the dirty floor, a flash of light and a familiar voice caught his attention.

He looked up and saw a console TV on a wheelie cart. The best time during class when everyone knew there was a movie about to be played. But there wasn't a movie on the screen; it was Alex.

Jacob got up and walked toward it. The screen was the brightest thing in the school, maybe even the current world. Jacob's eyes squinted, watching the screen. Alex was sitting at their normal lunch table in the cafeteria. But he was sitting with people Jacob didn't recognize.

The girl he sat with, a small blond girl with too-long hair and too much makeup, said, "Didn't you used to have a friend?" with a Southern twang. Alex was in the middle of drinking an apple juice.

"Yeah, but he couldn't handle life. A guy burned his homework, and he got sad and killed himself," he said with a chuckle at the end.

"People like that make me sick. Like, just get over it," the blonde girl said. The video zoomed out and showed the full cafeteria. Every kid and teacher turned their heads and stared at Jacob. He felt as though he were in the cafeteria with them. Alex raised from his seat and stared right into the camera; his face filled the old dusty television screen.

"Hmm, Jacob? Why'd you leave us? Your best friend that you were in love with, huh? Doesn't make much sense." Alex pulled his arm back and punched the screen, and it went black. The classroom went dark again. And Jacob was on the floor catching his breath.

Jacob went to try the door again, but he was still locked inside. He couldn't see out in the hallway anymore. It looked as though a wrestler was making an entrance. But he could smell burning.

The lockers exploded open, and flames shot out, surrounding the classroom. The thick fog seeped inside under the crack of the door, and Jacob ran to the windows. The glass panes were intact now, and he wasn't able to open them. He quickly grabbed a desk and dumped its contents onto the ground. Inside the desk slot erupted more red flames. He lifted it and tossed it at the window. It bounced off and rolled across the room, not doing any damage.

Jacob began hacking from the smoke and pounding on the windows. "Help! Somebody help me please!" he shouted. Outside standing in the grass area where they would have recess stood Alex. He was slowly moving his head from left to right.

"It's too late now. Love you, man," he said and walked off, disappearing into the fog. The smoke burned Jacob's eyes. And flames billowed out from every desk where each student held their books and supplies.

Jacob was now hacking, and he couldn't stop. He was clawing at his throat and gasping for air. Trying in any way he could to get oxygen. He laid on the ground since he remembered to get low as possible during a fire. This didn't work.

He got up and stumbled to the door once more but collapsed before reaching it. The door swung back open on its own. He climbed with his remaining strength to exit the classroom, but before he reached the door, the tiles collapsed beneath him, and he was falling again.

Chapter 16

It was like an instant replay. But now Jacob was in his room where he lived when his parents were together. The walls were a dark blue, and posters of his favorite superheroes were taped haphazardly. He was happy to see the mini drawing studio his mother and him had put together after their trip to Ikea. That time with her was more enjoyable than anything he had ever drawn. Drawings could be replaced, but time could not.

He wandered through the darkness of his old bedroom. He was still wearing the same shirt and shorts. His white socks remained darker than the hardwood floor he stood on.

When he exited his bedroom, he was relieved to not need to play the guessing game with doors again. But he was standing on the front cement stair that lead to the front yard of his old home. A prolonged shriek caught him off guard.

He followed the sound to his right on the side area of the house. It was his father raising a baseball bat down on his mother. Jacob ran toward him to catch his arms before they did damage. But he was stopped short and knocked to the ground. It was as though he walked into a pane-glass sliding door, but there was nothing there. He got up and banged on nothingness, but a bong sound vibrated back at him, and he realized it was a solid.

"Hey, Dad, please stop. Mom, get up. Please get up." Jacob wailed on the invisible fortress and cried out desperately.

"Hey, bud, how was school today? Better get started on your homework. Your Mom and I are just playing some baseball. You can't play with us because you're not around to play. So sad." His father had a crazed look in his eyes and a smile that would make the Joker proud.

"It's okay, sweetie. Don't listen to him. I could tell you were under a lot of pressure and you were in pain every day." Brenda was talking, lying on the ground with her face turned toward Jacob. "There is nothing wrong with what you did." Her face was soft, and all Jacob wanted to do was hold her.

The bat came down, and her face was still on him. Her head was being dented inward by multiple blows. Her left temple was like an in-ground pool of blood.

"Noooooo!" Jacob turned around, not being able to look and slid his back against the invisible wall and slid down. At the bottom, the solid wall disappeared, and now he lay on the ground, sobbing, staring into the empty black sky.

Bernie stood over him. Jacob got a full view of the bulge in his father's jeans.

"Get up, son. We got work to do." His father wandered off, and Jacob climbed to his feet without realizing it. He was pulling something now, something heavy. He looked behind him, and his unrecognizable mother was his wheelbarrow leaving behind a stream of blood.

"Throw her in," Bernie said with no remorse. Jacob dropped her legs and ran the opposite way.

When he reached the front yard, he was in the backyard again with his father standing there, his hands on his hips, waiting on Jacob to do what he'd asked. Jacob took different routes, even climbing fences and entering other homes that looked just as his home did. But he always ended up in his own backyard.

Reluctantly, as it would end the cycle, Jacob used all his will to shove his mother into the shed in the backyard. Her body was rag-dolled over the ride on mower. Bernie secured the shed with a lock and placed the key in his pocket.

Bernie walked back inside, humming a tune as though he had just finished yard work. Jacob was close behind him. He was going to go inside and get on the phone to call the police. Jacob ran up the back steps past his shithead father and raced to the dining room.

When Brenda would come home from work, she would always place her purse, keys, and cell phone on that table. Jacob walked into the room with the long brown table that had held family dinners for years until Bernie decided he didn't want to do that anymore. There were mountains of cell phones piled onto of one another. There were the old Nokia phones, Razer flip phones, and full touch-screen phones. Jacob picked up a small blue Nokia and dialed 911.

Holding it against his big head, the phone only came halfway down his face.

"911, what's your emergency?" a woman's tired voice asked.

Jacob opened his mouth to report the crime he'd just witnessed. But nothing came out. He was straining himself to talk, to scream. A vein bulged from his forehead, only air was coming out.

"Hello, anyone there? Are you in trouble and cannot talk? If this is this a crank call, you will be arrested."

Jacob imagined the lady filing her nails and chewing gum.

The phone line went dead, and Jacob's voice returned. He looked to the left, and his mother was standing in the mouth of the doorway that led to the kitchen. Her face was disoriented. Her eye looked ready to fall out of its socket. Dark blood rested on her cheeks and chin, and as she talked, her teeth were falling out.

"Oh, now you wanna talk. All those times I asked about your day and how you were doing, giving you the opportunity to ask for help. You always said you were fine. I knew you weren't fine or good or okay."

"Then why did…didn't you say anything," Jacob said between sobs.

"Because I can't do anything unless you say something. Just walking out the door of life ain't fix anything, did it?"

Jacob stared at the ground as he usually did when talking about how he felt. When he looked back up to respond, it was his father who was holding a gun, pointing the barrel at him. The Nokia dropped from his hand and surprisingly didn't break into pieces.

"I wouldn't make that call, son," he said and fired the weapon.

Jacob felt the force of the small bullet hit his chest and he was thrown backward into the nothing.

Chapter 17

The darkness flipped to light quickly. But it wasn't sunlight, it was more of a white light. It was as though he were trapped in a room with white walls and ceilings. There was a spot that looked to be a door handle, and Jacob turned it. It opened and a whoosh of powerful wind knocked him back onto his butt.

He was scared, and he gaped at the sight of a man with an orange suit and underwear on the outside with no genitals. It was Captain Ember. Jacob realized now, looking around, that he was in a comic book frame. The hero extended his arms, and flames shot out like from a flamethrower. Jacob rested his head on the floor—if you could call it a floor—to avoid the fiery snake.

When the captain ran off out of his view, shouting something inaudible, Jacob rose to his feet and peered out the opening to see inside. A long white hole dropped off in-between him and the vibrant colors of the action. He leaped the short distance and made it with ease.

He performed a somersault into the frame, and he was surrounded by large skyscrapers burning and people screaming in horror. But the hero that Jacob knew so well was nowhere to be found until Jacob found another opening. He leaped again with ease to find Ice Man inside a bank with a wall of ice for a doorway. Jacob touched the shimmering ice wall. It was cold.

"What is going on?" he said out loud to nobody. He looked to his right at the sound of screaming. The action had continued onto the next frame. He willed himself to not hesitate as he attempted to get ahead of the action. He leaped and landed on his feet for the first time. He ran through the fire-and-ice firing zone and could feel the heat radiating off the flame throwing.

He looked to his right and smiled at Captain Ember, remembering thinking him up while his parents were downstairs fighting. It was an escape into another world that made him the happiest he had ever been.

"Move out of the way, kid." Jacob didn't hear that—he read it. A white bubble with black text appeared above his head. Jacob looked to his right, and a dripping, clear-blue icicle missile was speeding toward him. He ducked and Captain Ember took it to the heart. Ember collapsed to the ground. Jacob raced over to help him but stopped. *No, go on to the next frame*, he told himself.

When he reached the next area, it was the first time it was peaceful. It was a downtown area bustling with cars and people. He heard laughs and cars honking in anger. Just a normal society. Then the ground was rumbling beneath his shoeless feet.

Ice Man had arrived riding on a wave of thick frost. It was as though the ocean had frozen and he was a surfer without a board. He must have been a hundred feet high, but he lowered to where Jacob was standing unable to move. Frozen.

"Where is your captain to save you now, Jacob." His eyes moved left and right, reading the dialogue bubble he had done in so many comic books before.

"He…he'll be here." Jacob noticed no bubble played above his head. Ice Man jumped down from his frozen wave and approached Jacob.

"Nah, I pierced his heart with a missile. Blood was spurting from his chest. And once again, you proved you cannot handle it. You ran off like the little baby you are." They were now standing chest to stomach. The blue-and-white mask that covered his hair, eyes, and nose looked different than what Jacob had remembered.

"You're not the real Ice Man," Jacob accused. He let out a bray laugh and pulled off the mask.

"Shit, you caught me," the man said as Jacob walked backward and ran into the door to the next frame.

"No, this is not real. This is not real," Jacob said as the door opened behind him, and he almost lost his balance, nearly falling into the pit of the unknown. He was looking at Robbie Stan, his school nemesis.

Robbie walked toward him with a feeling of power. He lifted his hands with palms up, and what looked to be a large ice cube floated in the air.

"Jacob" he heard somebody whispering. It was coming from behind him in the next frame. Jacob was happy to see Captain Ember there. Jacob bent his legs to jump to him. But Captain Ember put his hands in front of him.

"No, don't come over here. You will die if you do. You need to defeat him. It's the only way." After Jacob read the text bubble, it was too late to respond. The door had closed, and the handle disappeared. What he didn't notice was Robbie behind him ready to drop the ice cube on his head.

Jacob turned and pushed him with all his might. Robbie fell and so did the mega cube, breaking in half. Robbie used the power of his ice and raised it up without trying.

"That caught me off guard. You're usually a bitch who just sits there and takes it. But, no worries, I've got plenty more for ya."

Jacob didn't read past *bitch*. He only got up, feeling a heat flow through him. Like lava slowly dripping through his veins.

Jacob let out a rebel yell, and fire exited his mouth, imitating the mouth of a volcano. Lava flowed from his eyes and nose. He lifted his hands, and flames shot at Robbie. Robbie returned with a constant flow of thick ice. The ice was melting quickly, but it was constantly regenerating. Two strong forces meeting in the middle. But Jacob was being overpowered.

The blue frosty cylinder was slowly creeping toward him. He noticed this and used his will to push back. But it wasn't enough. Jacob was whacked in the face and dropped to the floor. He was lying on concrete, but it was cracking in a zigzag line beneath him. A piece of the black cement broke off, and he watched it fall until it was gone, which was where Jacob figured he was going next.

Robbie stood over him, and Jacob began to chuckle.

"What's so funny, loser?" the bubble popped up above his head.

"You have no balls, which depicts real life." Jacob could feel and hear the cracking sound of the ground beneath him crumbling.

"Real funny, shithead, but, hey, if you wanna go out laughing, be my guest." As Jacob read the speech bubble, the large ice cube formed in his hands. "Any last words?"

Jacob had the biggest grin he had ever had as he said, "You know, you always beat me up, said awful things to me, but I was always smarter than you."

Robbie let out a squealing laugh, like the sound when the teakettle is hot enough. Robbie released his hands, and the large ice cube was heading for Jacob's head. Jacob did a backward somersault and watched as the cube dropped through the cracked floor, Robbie falling right down with it.

Then Jacob was being lifted off his feet and felt as though he was being carried down…somewhere.

Chapter 18

Jacob floated down landing softly on his feet this time. He was standing inside his home again. The home he called his real home, when his mother and father lived there, and they were a family.

He was in his room, staring out the only window he had. Outside, the world was dark and gray, and it smelled like brimstone wafting through. His bed and desk seemed to have a graying tint surrounding them as well. The silence was deafening, and with each step he took, a creak echoed throughout his room.

He exited his room into the living room area. It finally was the living room and not a hallway of doors, only the doors that belonged. It was dark, but he could see where he was going. It was as though he had night vision goggles on.

His bedroom door slammed shut behind him, and he jumped. After that, the rest of the doors around him shut as well: his parents' room, the door to the kitchen, and the front door. The sliver at the bottom of the door to his parents' room had a beam of light passing through it every couple of seconds.

It reminded him of the lighthouse at Bayview Park. His dad took him there on his birthday every year. It was his favorite thing to walk out to on the boardwalk and lean on the edge, watching the water splash onto the rocks of the island where the lighthouse sat.

He was too nervous to open that door, so he went to the front door to exit. He wanted to just get out of the house and maybe head to Alex's because he would know what to do. He would know how to escape from this nightmare.

When he placed his hand on the round doorknob, an electric shock forced its way into his body and pulsated like he was experiencing a seizure for a few seconds. He fought through it and attempted to turn the handle, but it was locked. He fell to the wood floor and dried tears marked his cheeks as he screamed in pain. Then a scream came that was louder than his. He stopped and saw a shadow pass under the door to his parents' room. He slowly crawled to the room and reached up from the floor opening the door.

Inside was his parent's actual bedroom. His father stood over his mother with a baseball bat, the very same he'd seen his father with earlier, striking her head repeatedly.

Why am I seeing this again? Jacob thought. Blood shot up and splattered the walls and the bed. Jacob could tell she had been dead for a while. The blood had dried up on her already.

His father stopped hitting her as he crawled toward his mother. His face was splashed with lines of dark liquid. Bernie slowly moved his head from left to right, making a ticking sound through his teeth. Jacob had heard that noise and seen that face every time he did something his father did not approve of.

"You just couldn't mind your damn business ever, now could you?" his father said, walking toward him with the bat in his hand, shaking it, with both hands on the handle like a baseball player before stepping into the batter's box. The wet blood was flying off the tip of the barrel. "I gave you so much. But all you did was run back to your mother, you little fuck." He continued walking closer.

Jacob was on his ass, sliding back to the door that was shut now, holding out his arm in front of him.

"Please, Dad, I'm sorry. I loved y—I still love you," Jacob pleaded.

Bernie stopped at this, and the bat banged to the ground. Jacob watched as his father dropped to his knees. The wood floor shook through the soles of his shoes.

Face first, he hit the floor. Jacob knelt next to him to see if his father was okay. Jacob placed a consoling hand on his back, but his body was transparent, and his hand went down to the floor. Jacob drew his arm back in fear as Bernie began to cough and spoke in a tired, weak voice.

"I love you too, son."

Jacob wept over him tears fell off his cheeks. Like a river stream, they filled the gaps of each piece of hardwood and went underneath his father's still body.

Bernie Simeon then liquified into a puddle. The puddle moved toward Jacob and the door, not leaving a trail. He slipped under the door and vanished. Jacob quickly climbed to his feet and swung the door open.

He was back inside his bedroom now. This was a never-ending nightmare specifically made for Jacob. He had a queen-size bed with a Marvel Comics comforter that was half colored, the other half black outlines of various characters. He felt warm and safe under this heavy blanket. His mother came into his room every weekday morning to wake him by pulling them away from his face and kissing him gently on the forehead. He wished for that wet kiss right now.

He swung his feet to the floor and exited into the hallway. Other bedroom doors ran along the right side. The bathroom was the first on the right, and his parents' room was just beyond that. He reached the top of the stairs and heard sharp breaths echoing from downstairs. It sounded like someone sobbing. Jacob carefully descended the stairs with his hand gliding on the wooden handrail. At the bottom, he followed the sound to the right and into the kitchen.

His mother was at the table where they would have family dinner every night. Her hands were over her eyes, and her sobbing was inconsolable.

"Mom?" he said as he entered the white kitchen. He could feel the cold tile floor through his socks.

She snapped her head toward him. "I can't believe he's gone," she said. "My baby is gone, and it's all your fault." She pointed at him. Jacob looked behind him to see the empty dark hallway of the front door entrance area.

"Mom, I'm right here. Mom." Jacob waved his hand at his mother's blank stare.

"He was the only one I had in my life, the only one I could talk to about anything, the only person I loved." Jacob slowly walked toward her shuffling his feet on the tiles. "Why did you leave?" she said, pulling a long bottle of clear liquid out and wrapping her lips around it. Bubbles gurgled with each gulp she consumed.

"I didn't leave you; I swear, Mom. I'm right here, please. I need you, Mom. I'm scared and I have no one." As he approached with his hands out in front of him to embrace her, his mother pulled a handgun from her lap and faced Jacob.

"I love you, kiddo. And it's okay to feel scared. It's okay to feel lonely. It's a part of life." She smiled, placed the gun to her temple and pulled the trigger.

"No, Mom," he said, leaping on her to pull her arm back, but his head bounced off the bench on which she sat. Crimson red covered his entire body, and his mother was gone. He banged his fists on the bench in which they shared family meals and then climbed back to his feet and ran to the front door, stepping onto the mat that read Welcome Home. The blood was running over his face, covering his eyes and mouth. He could taste a certain sweetness from the blood and saltiness from his tears.

The outside was dark, and he could barely see through the thick blood, but he could only make out silhouettes.

They were suspended high in the air. *Must be over a hundred feet*, Jacob thought.

Jacob wiped his eyes and the mess from his face. When he opened them, he could see neat rows of people about ten across and went back as far as he could see. In the front row was his family—his father, his mother, his aunts, and his best friend, all of them hanging with thick brown rope around their necks and motionless.

Jacob fell backward and hit his backside on the welcome mat. He looked away and stood, opening the door to go back inside, to maybe go to his room and hide, but the inside was the outside, an exact replica either way he went.

He stepped through, and a voice was behind him. "Hey, kid," the deep voice muttered. He slowly turned to see a well-dressed man with a clean-shaved face and wearing a military uniform with badges shining on his chest. "Remember me?" The man spread his arms and smiled. Jacob stared at him for a few seconds with a slight recognition but slowly shook his head.

The man scrunched down a bit and walked with a limp and made his face angry looking. "Got any money, kid?" he said, mimicking himself.

Jacob recognized him as the dirty homeless man who'd chased him for money. And his face must've shown it.

"Ah, there you go. I knew you'd get there."

"But you look so young now, sorry."

The man laughed as though Jacob had told him the best joke. "We are as we perceive people, wouldn't you say?"

The man seemed to be of good wisdom, and the only thing Jacob could think to ask was, "Are you God?"

The man belly laughed again for a longer time. "If only. But does this look like heaven to you?"

Jacob thought this was a rhetorical question, but the man was waiting for an answer. "No. But why would I go to hell?" Jacob asked curiously.

"Hey, look, kid, I'm not the religious type, so I'm not the one you want ask questions about that stuff to. What I can do is tell you a story." Story was the one thing Jacob lacked in his comics but loved to listen and read them.

"I was in the Marine Corps, as you can probably tell, for thirteen years, and I had a buddy I served with all those years. We were on every mission together. We saw some serious shit. Our own men getting their brains blown from their skulls. We blew brains from the enemies' skulls. But one thing we did have was each other's backs until the day we died. Well, to make a long story longer, we moved in together, and he got a job with the DOT."

Jacob furrowed his brows and tilted his head.

"The people on the highway that cut the trees and plow the snow in the orange trucks."

Jacob nodded and he continued.

"Anyhow, he was paying for an apartment we were sharing, and one day at the job, they were cutting and shredding up tree trunks on the side of the highway. And he…well, he just kind of did his best pool dive into the shredder."

The man looked up into the dark sky. There was a single dot of light burning, and the man smiled.

"Later on, when cleaning out his room I found a journal he had kept and read every single page. It went all the way back to our last day in the military. It gave me an inside look into his mind, and he was looking to leave this world for a while. But I'm not telling you this for the purpose of sympathy or how there are lives worse than yours. While I died from a heart attack, I understand how depression works. But the point of all this blabbering is that if he had talked to me about this, I would have held him in my arms so he couldn't go to work that day or go anywhere where he could harm himself. And I know the people you love love you back and would do the same for you."

Jacob was still covered in blood, but dried up, over his clothing. He looked up at the man and asked, "So, that's why you sent me that message? Why you said that to me on my way to school?"

The man smiled. "Correctamundo, my good friend."

"But haven't I already done that? Isn't it too late?" Jacob asked worried.

"I wouldn't get ahead of yourself just yet. Let me explain what I know. Before, you asked me where we were. We are inside of you." The man paused and coughed away a laugh. "What I mean is we are inside your mind. And I honestly don't even know why I'm here, but I've been here a while and sneak into the 'real world' sometimes. To warn people of their approaching deaths. Apparently, there are many people like me."

Jacob had so many questions for the man.

"Wait, so who are you then? The gatekeeper?" Jacob asked.

"I guess I would be your conscience and the conscience of many. And each of the people you face every day has helped you along your journey of life so far. Your best friend is your realist, your father is your evil, and your mother is your kindness. You've got a lot of the latter."

"Then what is Robbie?" Jacob wondered.

"Ah, yeah he is your fear, depression, and everything bad that sits in your head. And you overcame part of it. Those things will be with you forever, but you made a giant leap. And you know what that means, don't you?"

Jacob stood there looking up at the people in his life all hanging from ropes, just as he had. "No." Jacob said, and the old man began walking away.

"Hey where are you going? And what does it mean?" Jacob shouted.

"I'm always around, and you will soon find out." The old man disappeared into the fog, leaving Jacob on the doorstep looking up at his family and friend again, but they were gone now. It was only empty nooses swaying in the faint breeze.

He felt a sense of relief. He felt regenerated, ready to take on whatever came to him. As he peered into the sky, a bolt of lightning came down and struck him on the chest. He kept his balance, but it hurt like hell. Another bolt came down, and he was now floating upward, struck with the bolts every few seconds.

"What the hell is happening?" he said to nobody.

He was passing through white puffy clouds and images of him with his mother appeared. Memories of her holding him and loving him through all the years until she was taken from him.

"I love you, baby." He heard echo through his ears. Then he dropped.

***

The ache in his back was unbearable, but not as bad as his neck. And his chest was burning. But he was in a comfortable position.

He was laying prone in a white-sheeted bed. He looked down to see round sticky pads on his chest. Jacob scanned

the room he was in. White walls surrounded him, and so
did men in white coats. *Doctors*, Jacob thought.

"Hey, good morning, Jacob. You've been sleeping for a
bit," the man in the white coat said in an excited way.

"Ah," Jacob attempted to speak.

"No, save your breath, buddy. You're pretty banged up,
so don't move a muscle. We've put your neck in a brace, so
it will be a bit uncomfortable. I'm Dr. Lafaille, and you're
in Greenville Hospital, and you're going to be okay."

Jacob felt weak. He tried moving his arm up, but it
stayed on the ground.

He opened his mouth, and a squeak exited through his
dry, cracked lips. "You have some concerned family
members outside waiting to see you. Blink once if I can
send them in. Blink twice—"

Jacob closed his eyes and squeezed them and opened
them and kept them open.

"Very well then. Send the family in, please, nurse."

Alex was first through the door with his arms stretched
out. His aunt followed behind. They looked to have been
crying for a long while. Which was unusual because Jacob
had never seen Alex cry in all time he'd known him.

"Yo, man, you scared the hell out of me, bro. I went to
your house because I didn't want you to think I was mad at
you, and I took you down. You weren't breathin' and I did
the chest-pushing thing. And I put my lips on you, bro. To

breathe into your mouth, of course. I learnt that from Mr. Benivo's health class. I mean I'm not sure if I did anything to help, but you know—"

"Okay, let's give his brain a break. It's already been through enough," Aunt Carrie said pulling Alex back from the bed. Aunt Carrie gave Jacob's forehead a wet kiss, the kisses he missed so much from his mother.

They walked out with Alex still telling his heroic story. And as Jacob lay there, Alex returned. Jacob expected Alex to tell him something Alex had forgotten.

"I love you, man," he said. This surprised Jacob, and he grabbed his hand for a few seconds. Then he caught up with Aunt Carrie outside the room, and the door closed.

Chapter 19

The smell of fresh buttery popcorn reached his room, which was on the same floor as the kitchen. Jacob loved his new bedroom where he could hang whichever posters he liked and had a comforter he was warm underneath. But, most importantly, he had Aunt Carrie tucking him in and giving him good-night kisses and hugs every night.

It was more difficult for Jacob to draw with the neck brace since it forced his head up, but his redrawing of his Captain Ember comic was coming along great.

In the living room, Alex was already waiting for him on the couch.

"Auntie Carrie, it's starting! Hurry up!" Jacob yelled, exiting his room and plopping on the couch.

"I'll be there in a second sweetheart. Just start without me," she replied. The fluttering of pages indicated a Marvel movie was beginning on the television. Jacob bounced up and down on the cushion.

Alex lay a hand on his shoulder. "Hey, not too much bouncing, my man." Jacob smiled at Alex's concerned face.

"I've got my trusty brace to hold me in place. But I appreciate your concern always. Does everyone miss me at school?" He smiled in his brace.

"I don't know, but I sure do, man." He hugged his friend from the side, and Alex patted him with his free hand.

"Whatever happened to Robbie?"

"Oh yeah, I forgot to tell you. He got expelled." The excitement went up to a squeal in Alex's voice. "They looked over the footage of him burning—" Alex stopped.

"Burning my comic," Jacob finished for him.

"Yeah, and of him bullying a bunch of other kids. I heard a rumor that he might be arrested for breaking this kid's arm," Alex explained and Jacob smiled, remembering the relief he'd felt when he'd defeated Robbie inside the comic book.

"Okay, buttered movie theater popcorn fresh from the micro—I mean, the popcorn machine we have in the basement," Auntie Carrie said entering the living room with a large glass bowl. The boys both looked at her with disbelieving eyes.

"All right, all right, it's microwave popcorn, but it's the best brand there is."

They shot her the same look, and they fell out laughing together. She placed the bowl on the table between the television and the hungry boys. They both stepped off the couch and reached their claws into the bowl, and the white puffs flew all over the table and the carpet. Auntie Carrie opened her mouth to scold them but couldn't see past their smiling faces to do so.

They were lucky enough to catch a rare broadcast of the first *Iron Man* movie on CBS. Jacob was upset since *Avengers: Endgame* was in theaters and his aunt hadn't taken him to see it yet. She said when maybe when it came out on DVD.

As Tony Stark was telling the soldier to not put up gang signs Auntie Carrie reclined in her rocker, watching Jacob and Alex laugh and toss popcorn into the air, attempting to catch it in their mouths. The convoy in front of Tony Stark and the soldiers exploded into a fireball, and all three of them jumped. Jacob rubbed the back of his head.

"Ow."

"Are you okay?" his aunt said, pulling the recliner lever up.

"Yeah, I think I just jumped too hard," Jacob replied. The hail of gunfire on the television was interrupted by the sound of the news broadcast sound and "Breaking News" in block letters floating across the screen like an Adobe Flash feature.

A handsome news broadcaster sat at a desk and said, "We interrupt your current broadcast schedule for a breaking news bulletin." It was the local news network of Greenville. A video began to play of Bernie Simeon exiting the downtown courthouse using a tan suit jacket draped in front of his face to hide from the flashing blue bulbs that surrounded him. Carrie grabbed the remote from the side table.

"Let's watch something else," she said. An emphatic "*No!*" came from the couch. Jacob was holding out his arm with his palm facing his aunt. Alex sat beside him in silence.

"Bernie Simeon from here in Greenville was accused of the murder of his wife, Brenda Simeon, who was found beaten by a blunt object and stuffed into the shed in her own backyard," the newscaster went on.

"We don't need to watch this." Auntie Carrie said, the remote shaking in her hand. She peeked over at Jacob who had his arm still extended and tears were dropping like rain off his chin.

"Bernie is the father of the boy people are calling 'Miracle Child,' Jacob Simeon, who survived a suicide attempt—" The television screen flashed, and a woman and a man were selling NFL jackets with each team's logo on the individual jackets.

"Call now. This offer won't last forever," the woman on the TV said in a Southern drawl.

"Change it back," Jacob said, not looking at his aunt.

"You really shouldn't be watching that." Her voice was shaky. She sounded scared of him. His eyes looked to be tiny balls of fire, and he stood up, walking toward her. He snatched the remote from her hands and changed it back.

"…Simeon was found not guilty today of murder," the broadcaster informed the camera. The shot of his father leaving the courthouse ran on loop a few more times, and the broadcaster said they were returning to the regularly scheduled programming. The movie cut back on to in time for Iron Man to come onto the screen with the title shot and a hammer-hitting-iron sound.

Jacob just sat there frozen. The remote dropped out of his hand and smashed on the hardwood floor. The batteries flew across the room toward the front door and rolled to a stop there. Jacob jumped off the couch and ran outside, slamming the front door.

"I'll go check on him," Auntie Carrie said to a stunned Alex, who was staring at Iron Man on the TV.

She opened the door to see the back of Jacob's head. She slowly approached him from behind but made enough noise to let him know she was there. She sat next to him on the front step, looking out into the half-dark sky over the residential neighborhood. Carrie placed an arm around Jacob and squeezed. The feel of the tough neck brace on her forearm. Alex strolled onto the steps after her sitting on the other side of Jacob.

"Your father did some bad things, but—"

"No," Jacob muffled through his hands. "He wasn't a good man who did bad things. He was just a bad man. I just wish my mom saw that sooner."

"Hey, we don't need to talk about th—," Aunt Carrie said but Jacob was only shaking his head.

"Keeping silent hurts people. I want to talk about it."

Jacob began to talk about everything that had happened, and he didn't stop.

www.ingramcontent.com/pod-product-compliance
Lightning Source LLC
Chambersburg PA
CBHW061456210726
48287CB00007B/2534